D0088971

SUCH
a Pretty
FACE

EDITED BY **ANN ANGEL**

Amulet Books

New York

SUCH a Pretty FACE

SHORT STORIES
about Beauty

This is dedicated to the writers within
for sharing their beautiful passion.

—Ann Angel

Contents

Beauty I'd always missed
With these eyes before

—The Moody Blues, "Nights in White Satin"

INTRODUCTION

Ann Angel

My older sister Katie raced into her teens with a head full of crazy dark curls and wild blue eyes that warned she would take on anyone and win them over. She had looks and charm and fascinating, sometimes insane, ideas. She was the pretty girl whom all the other girls wanted to be. The guys swarmed around her like bees seeking honey. And if sometimes they seemed more like lusty dogs hungry for action, Katie was able to make them believe there was a chance without really giving them one. She was the party girl, the fun one, the beautiful sister I also wanted to be, but there were times I thought she was my tormentor.

I slunk into my own teens furtively, aware that guys failed to see me when I walked down the school halls. The girls only wanted to be around me to get near my popular big sister. Born slightly less than a year after Katie, I was the short "Irish twin" whose hair hung straight and lank. My own serious blue eyes were usually hidden behind the pages of a notebook, where I wrote snippets of stories and bad poetry.

Katie was quick to tell me I was a dork, a nerd. Too smart for guys to like. Too shrimpy for guys to think I was anything more than a kid. Too unaware to be cool.

I followed our unwritten rule, that I could talk only to those girls who weren't already Katie's friends. I had one of those. She had all the rest.

I felt little-girl blue next to my sister's dark beauty. Katie wore tight jeans and sexy silk shirts that all the girls copied, the sleeves of which all the boys loved to slide their hands along. My broadcloth shirts hung on me, and I only owned one pair of jeans.

Katie and her friends seemed always to know whose parents were gone, where the party was. While

I spent Friday nights babysitting, I imagined the group I thought of as "the beautiful girls" sipping stolen liquor out of pickle jars, pairing up, and kissing boys.

Even if the topic of the next party came up in front of me, I was never invited. Had I shown up at a party, I knew the beautiful girls would have entertained themselves watching the boys pass by invisible me.

So I should have known something was up when one of the beautiful boys, a curly-haired football player named Jay* with deep brown eyes, showed up one night while I was babysitting my younger siblings. I invited him in to watch a movie. I can't tell you what it was about—I only noticed he sat so close that the heat of his leg seared my thigh. I glued my eyes to the television screen. I remember pulling away a bit but missing the feel of him and letting my knee fall back toward his. I kept feeding my baby sister her bottle.

I burped my sister and took her to her crib. I tucked her in, certain Jay would be gone when I returned to the family room. But he was still sitting there, watching the movie.

*Some names have been changed.

I considered moving to a chair but didn't want him to think I was as dorky as I knew I was. So I sat on the couch a little bit away from him.

Jay moved in. Put his arm around my shoulders. I stared at that screen as though it could swallow me, feeling the weight of his thick arm, thinking this was too cool, wondering if my face was turning red.

I had no idea what to say. I had no idea why he suddenly liked me. But I was glad he did.

I turned to tell Jay that my parents would be home soon.

He turned too.

We locked lips.

He smelled of English Leather and that warm wool smell that permeates letter jackets. I loved that kiss. In fact, I kissed him again. And again. And, why not? Again.

When we heard the garage door open, we jumped apart.

"I gotta go," he said.

I didn't notice that he failed to say, "I'll call you." He didn't look back at me as I followed him to the kitchen door. And I was too tongue-tied with his kisses to speak, so in love with his mouth and brown eyes. My mind spun with my luck! I imagined he'd call the next day. We'd go to a party the next week. My storyteller's mind floated into a perfect future.

I was convinced Jay was my prince, my ticket to popularity, my ride out of the world of nerdy people. I showed him out the back door just before my parents walked through the front. I went to bed that night one happy little dreamer.

The next day I waited for a call. It didn't come. I told Katie what had happened. And when she didn't seem happy for me, I was sure she was jealous.

On Monday at school, when the beautiful girls gathered in the bathroom after lunch to discuss the weekend, I was in there with them. My sister's side-kick, Sue, asked me about my weekend. I told her about Jay. First Maura, then Sheila, Barb, and Patty turned to listen to me. I was the center of attention as I told the popular girls about my wonderful night.

My sister Katie remained uncharacteristically silent.

Before I finished my story, she turned so quietly that not a single curl swayed, and walked out the door.

It was after supper that night that she came into my room and told me, "Sue paid Jay to kiss you. It was a joke." Her eyes flashed anger at me when she added, "They were all laughing about you."

I was frozen in place. While I stood there paralyzed, a rage so wild filled me, I wanted to slap her silly. I hated her for telling me the truth, and for failing to have the power to stop her friends. I reached out, grabbed her hand, and wove my fingers between hers. I squeezed until I saw pain in her splendid eyes.

Then I hugged her and cried into her shoulder while she held on tight, as only a sister who loves you can.

I doubt I slept much that night. I know that sometime before the next morning I figured it out. Being beautiful doesn't make a person all-powerful, and it doesn't make a person good. Those girls flocked to my sister, but it seemed she couldn't control them or protect me from them. And I saw that their power to hurt me came from my own misplaced regard for them and their looks.

I recall that a blush burned my cheeks when I faced those girls the next day. But I walked tall and alone. When Sue asked me how Jay was, I stared straight into her eyes and didn't bother to answer. When Maura asked me if he'd called, I only smiled. As I looked into each face, I saw how ugly they had made themselves to me.

When I ran into Jay in the hall, I looked into those brown eyes, and though I wanted to, I didn't call him an ass. I just smiled until he blushed. I said, "I know they paid you five dollars to kiss me."

He looked down and mumbled, "I'm sorry. I didn't take the money." That evening he called me and apologized again.

Though we dated for a while after that, his kisses had lost their magic. But beauty was redefined in my life for ever after. For me, beauty comes from the goodness of a person's heart or soul, not a person's physical characteristics. I will always carry the knowledge that those girls, and others like them, aren't beautiful people. I can't be either if I let them have power over me.

And so, the stories included in this collection look beyond the pretty face to the person within. They examine the wonderful, and sometimes wretched, ways beauty exists around us. Some of the stories on these pages examine the ideal of physical beauty, some define beauty found in nature and emotion, and others respond to beauty's absence.

While some of these stories acknowledge our culture's obsession with looks, the writers refuse to accept beauty's myths. In honestly examining beauty, these authors make connections to something deeper—a beauty of the heart and soul.

I hope their stories help you to redefine beauty, to recognize that beauty is so much more than the almost impossible physical ideal we've come to worship. Beauty can be a friend who knows when to sit quietly by our side. It can be found in nature or in a stunning moment of self-recognition. Beauty can be found in one special person who knocks the breath from you because he or she is honest and unique.

Maybe we need to reach our own conclusions about what is beautiful and give beauty breadth and scope, so we'll always find something to celebrate in ourselves and those around us.

As you move from story to story, I think you'll experience a surprising range of emotions evoked by the unexpected insights that fill these pages. In the first story, Ron Koertge's "Such a Pretty Face," we see that even the most physically beautiful have rules to live by. From here, the stories move to subtle and more personal perspectives on beauty, captured in a significant moment of meaning.

Mary Ann Rodman suggests that none of us are good enough when we measure ourselves against the collective ideal of beauty. Chris Lynch's "Red Rover, Red Rover" asks if judging others based on the physical is a shallow view. Lauren Myracle's hilarious story, "Bad Hair Day," demonstrates the mistake of focusing on our flaws, no matter how insistently they demand our attention. Louise Hawes's story, "Sideshow," depicts rejection in the extreme, exploring what happens when we fail to measure up in the eyes of someone we wish to emulate.

Many of these stories depict characters in situations that unravel their beliefs about beauty and leave them with a deeper understanding of what they value in the world. Jamie Pittel's "What I Look Like" talks about how we find our own beauty and how we come to really *own* our beauty. Rather than in the mirror, J. James Keels suggests, we find our beauty reflected in someone close to us. While Ellen Wittlinger's "Cheekbones" shows the possibility of escape from a beauty trap, Norma Fox Mazer's "How to Survive a Name" makes it clear that sometimes beauty is nothing more than a name.

Tim Wynne-Jones shows us how we can look at the world to see beauty. Anita Riggio follows the lives of two teens: one who sees no beauty in life, and his best friend, who sees beauty all around her. Finally, Jacqueline Woodson plays on the theme that beauty can be discovered outside our physical selves. It is found in personality, in community, in the world, and in our independent values.

Introduction

This collection is intended to challenge our culture's emphasis on appearance, the message that our physical self is more important than our intellect and sensibility.

May you discover, like the characters on these pages, that we aren't just pretty faces. We're individuals who define beauty through our lack of uniformity and conformity, through our intellect and uniqueness, through our enthusiasm, humor, energy, and independence.

I hope this collection encourages you to search for new and individual awareness of beauty in your life. I hope this journey moves you to discover that beauty goes beyond the physical to encompass all of the unique aspects that make up this beautiful, crazy world.

SUCH a Pretty FACE

Ron Koertge

A DAY AT THE BEACH WITH BEAUTY

Melissa always has a convertible, but her classmates pile into old VWs and Volvo station wagons with dents. In the movies, a beautiful girl has a spunky chum who hooks up with the handsome guy's goofy buddy so they can all double-date. But Melissa has never had that sort of confidante. When kids do hitch a ride, they talk around her. Over and around. Rarely to. Maybe it's because she's always busy with other drivers. Men who throw their business cards at her. Or hold up hastily printed signs that proffer and cajole. It's always a relief to get where she's going. To see the coolers, the gaily striped chairs that unfold, the faithful volleyball. Because somebody might toss her a Frisbee, ask her to start a fire, or want to race to the nearest lifeguard's stand. They might, but they don't. Melissa watches the others sprawl on the sand. Boys start a fire, order one another around. Girls put sunblock on one another. A ponytail nestles into the nearest lap. Or across the small of a back. Or on a nicely upholstered buttock. Tiny radios appear, like books that gossip and sing. Laptops with DVDs yield stories of violence and passion, secrecy and love. Someone opens the contraband beer, lights a joint. Melissa sips bottled water. She's accepted without being ostracized, segregated but not expelled. She tries to believe her friends are protecting her. They might say, "Melissa wouldn't like that. It's not her. But she's cool." They might, but they don't. Everybody swims while the coals die down. They dive and horse around, then burst out of the surf, trunks tugged low by gravity, hair mashed flat or shaped by an energetic hand into quills. Their knees are knobby, stomachs a little slack, a bruised thigh here, a bristly armpit there. Melissa swims alone, emerges from the spindrift bejeweled. She appears groomed by the ocean, not disheveled. As she approaches, headphones go on, music's turned up. She passes among them, passes through them. No one offers her a chili dog, some Doritos, or a beer. No one makes a space for her on their messy towels. She reaches her blanket, perfectly square and unsoiled, and settles into the lotus pose, eyes fixed on the couple beside her locked in a pythonlike embrace.

3

BEAUTY BUYS A WART

Melissa knows about shops like Costume Heaven; they flourish every year around Halloween, and the owners manage to eke out a living the rest of the time selling fake blood, sneezing powder, and whoopee cushions to nine-year-old boys. What doesn't surprise Melissa is how what is grotesque and ugly outnumbers (and outsells!) what is comely. For every Snow White wig and tube of alabaster makeup, there are dozens of pimples and warts, rubber fungi, giant proboscises, bloodshot eyes, and scruffy wigs. Melissa settles for a small kit, wart + wart glue: $1.98. Her girlfriends whisper one to another, "What does she—of all people—need with a Melissa mark?" So she goes to a different aisle and buys a big snout + snout strap: $3.50. Her friends just stare at her, but crack up when one of the guys slips on the Dangling Eyeball Glasses. Melissa buys a Nixon mask, the rubber one, and wears it to school. Her friends are not amused. In fact, they're nonplussed. Even her teachers act concerned. "Take that thing off." She does, because Melissa is obedient.

BEAUTY GOES SHOPPING

She only needs a few things, so she drives to the nearest upscale department store. A man about to park right near the entrance gives up his spot; the doorman adjusts his gold epaulets, elbows two or three customers out of the way, and bows as she passes. Salespeople stop gossiping, folding, and straightening. A frock is pressed up against her and at just that, without her even trying it on, the employees burst into spontaneous applause and half a dozen customers demand exactly that dress in exactly that color and size and press it against them too, please. Melissa buys a pair of gloves, and everyone watching buys a similar pair. Next Melissa purchases Ginger Body Crème & Lotion. Two or three tame boyfriends who joined Melissa's entourage have to sit down and fan themselves after watching her rub lotion on her forearms and wrists. The stuff sells out in a twinkling, and one savvy man calls his broker and buys Ginger Inc. She wishes they wouldn't do that, but she can't stop them. Then Melissa glides through the makeup department and is entreated by the pearly servants of Dior. They long to apply their unguents, antidotes, and balm. They begin to fight over her, so Melissa agrees, lest a riot break out. She perches on a tall stool. Kathleen (her nametag says so) pops in a breath mint and begins. Melissa can't help but notice some friends of hers from Honors English sitting nearby with a startling eye and a drab one, a rosy cheek and a pale one, half a sanguine lip. "Finish them," Melissa says. Kathleen barely glances. "Oh, they can wait."

5

"But I insist." Kathleen leans in. "Don't be that way," she implores. "I'm not really doing anything to you. I wouldn't gild the lily; I'm just pretending. But look at this crowd! They don't know that. And the minute you leave, I'll sell thousands of dollars' worth of product. I'll be merchant of the month!" Melissa looks at her school chums. "This isn't my fault." "Oh," says the Luminous Eye, "it's never your fault, is it?" Pale Cheek tears off a protective bib and stomps away. "You bitch," cries one voluptuous Scarlet Lip, the other achromatic and thin.

BEAUTY GOES TO THE DOCTOR

Sometimes she has to. Before a contest. Or a trip overseas with her chaperone. Nothing's ever wrong, yet there's something disquieting about the appointment. Could it be the drive? She's been chauffeured before, lots of times. And there's always something trifling about the backseat. Like someone might hand her a book of simple puzzles or a doll while those up front drive and discuss important things. At the medical plaza she signs in, takes a seat. Women in bright smocks filter out from the back and peer at her. Other doctors, stethoscopes hanging around their necks like tame adders, muse: *To examine Melissa. To take Melissa's pulse. Listen to Melissa's heart.* For a while she looks around, notices how those with prosperous skin sit on one side of the room facing the infected and feverish. A toddler careens into her arms. How unambiguous babies are! Melissa thinks how everyone else is in disguise, full of tricks and lies. Is she? Time to flip through a magazine. Any magazine. Even a medical journal. She ponders a section of epidermis: stratum corneum, stratum lucidum, stratum granulosum, stratum Malpighii, stratum germinativum. She wonders at which stratum Melissa stops if it is only skin deep? And what about the cooperation of the organs, efficient glands, orgy of digestion. Nothing calculated, selfish, or underhanded there. Isn't that beautiful? And if so, is everyone beautiful inside? Again she vows to do more with her life. To puzzle things out. Read deeply. Think hard. "The doctor will see you now." A beaming nurse holds open a beige door. Melissa is glad to see him.

Intelligent him. Educated him. Wise him. "I might," she blurts, "go to medical school, too." "No one," he says, "looks adorable in that gown but you." "I know I could get in. My grades are excellent." "Deep breath, please. And hold." "I'd like to help people. I'd like to do something useful." "Say 'Ahhh.'" "Are you listening, doctor? Have you heard a word I said?" "Hmm. Your pulse is a little rapid. Any unusual stress in your life lately?"

BEAUTY GOES TO THE MUSEUM

It's a field trip with her art teacher, Ms. Perspective. Their bus is long and sleek with a jagged bolt of lightning on the side, the bus driver slim-hipped in his blue uniform with stripes on the cuffs. Melissa's seatmate is tongue tied. He can only nod when Melissa makes small talk. He does manage to stutter that this is a day he'll never forget. But Melissa is only embarrassed by her enormous unearned power. Ashamed of it almost. She's looking forward to the museum. Melissa is surprised to see Ms. Perspective not worshiping a van Gogh but flirting

with the driver. She watches her classmates pair off.
One couple starts to sketch. The class clown whips
out a beret and starts chattering in faux French. She
wanders down a well-lit corridor, past a guard or two
in sensible shoes and one-size-fits-none blazers. She
takes in the first still life: a bouquet of carnations,
two pomegranates, one silver letter opener. Melissa
leans closer. A ladybug clings to a stem, light reflects
off its folded wings. On the letter opener's blade
stands a single drop of water like a tiny, transparent
igloo. Melissa moves on to clear goblets of red wine,
a pheasant, and a hare. "Both dead," intones her
teacher. "The necks loose and suddenly elderly, but
their feathers and fur still lustrous and incorruptible."
Guess what Melissa found in the mirror not five
hours ago: a line on her brow. A line that wasn't there
last week. The kind of line that becomes a wrinkle or
at least foreshadows one, like the crack in the dam
that alerts the reader to the final chapter's flood.
Someday will she be demoted from Beautiful to
Lovely, from Lovely to Good-Looking, from Good-
Looking to Still-Pretty-For-Her-Age? Her teacher

9

clearly envies the statues' marble obstinacy, their enduring thighs. She's jealous of that ladybug, forever red and black, forever at home on that vigorous, nearly immortal stem. But in a way, Melissa welcomes the flaws, each one a ticket to the world of the majority.

BEAUTY HAS AMNESIA

She wakes up in a hospital with a bandage on her forehead. "Where am I?" The voice is pleasing and melodious, but whom does it belong to? The plastic bracelet on her arm says Jane Doe. She presses the call button. "Oh good," the nurse says. "You're awake. How do you feel?" "Peculiar. Disembodied. Not myself, whoever that is." "Well, it shouldn't be long now before we find out. Your picture is in the paper; we're getting lots of calls from people claiming to be your parents. People with deep voices, curiously enough." "How did I get here?" "Do you remember being at the football game? The pigskin spiraling toward you? Tumbling from the stands?" "Actually, no." Nurse pats her hand. "Could you eat a little something?" "What would someone like me eat?"

"Probably ambrosia, tongues of nightingales, caviar. But what we have is Jell-O." "Do I like Jell-O?" "Why don't we find out?" What a good idea! This is how she'll discover her identity, by likes and dislikes. Jell-O—yes or no? Football—not likely. This gown that opens in the back—no way. This nurse is pleasing, but others might not be. On TV, someone is weeping: no. A pretty girl sitting in a meadow gazing fondly at a sanitary napkin: maybe. A sleek automobile on a closed course with a professional driver: looks like fun. Just then the door opens and a crowd of deliverymen surges in. Most with metallic GET WELL SOON balloons. Flowers of all kinds. A stuffed animal as big as a bear. Is a bear, actually. But softer and much less dangerous. A nurse plucks cards, begins to read. " 'Hurry back, Melissa. We need you. Who will be Melissa Queen, Prom Melissa, Valentine's Melissa, Harvest Melissa, Melissa of Winter Carnival, Melissa of the Glorious Fourth, and so on.' " "That's who you are," says the nurse. "I should have guessed." "So I'm Melissa?" The nurse waves the cards around. "Well, everyone certainly says so."

BEAUTY IS HOME ALONE
WHEN THE POWER FAILS

There's nothing to be afraid of. It's midafternoon. And anyway, a delightful coolness falls across the house. The heartless cat (the way he brings in sparrows and lays them at her feet as if she were a goddess) pads by to get a drink of water, collapses by the blue bowl, goes back to sleep. The dog moves closer, looks up eagerly. Melissa remembers when these pets would accompany her on imaginary adventures, all of them sitting up on her bed, which could fly, banking left or right depending on which way she leaned, and carrying them toward teeming jungles, dens of pirates, and the Haunted Forest. Melissa wonders what became of those journeys. She was awfully cute then. Merely cute. Just another Terrific Tot. Regularly driven to dance class, gymnastics class, singing lessons. And then Junior Miss. After which she left her magic bed behind. Abandoned her animal friends to their own devices. She stared out the car window. Smiled politely at those who gawked and sometimes put on their sunglasses as if she were luminous. Now the TV is dark. Her radio silent as a brick. Melissa wanders to the windows, peeks between venetian blinds. The woman next door has a child about five. Melissa can see them sitting at a sunny table, coloring together. Each has a book of her own. Each chooses from the enormous box of crayons, removing Burnt Sienna or Atomic Tangerine as swiftly as a highwayman drawing his sword. Melissa remembers coloring: Once she made a farmer blue, a spaniel green, two cows red as sores. Then she went outside the lines: Flesh tones lapped onto the hedge, sky trickled into a station wagon, bark leapt from the tree onto a nearby swan. "Oh no," someone said. "Melissa is as Melissa does." Melissa liked being bad. Was thrilled by it. But she did as she was told. Of course. Now in the shadowed, shadowy house she wonders what might have happened if she'd persisted. Was there such a thing as a beautiful anarchist? A lovely troublemaker? In the teeming jungle her favorite animal was the warthog. On Pirate Island she had a peg leg. In the Haunted Forest she consorted with hags, laughing at human vanity and never brushing her

13

teeth. Just then power is restored. On TV a couple embraces, the radio bemoans congestion in Arcadia. Many lights are on. She can see herself in the mirrors again: here, there, everywhere. And always completely inside the lines.

BEAUTY MAKES A MISTAKE

Love letters turn up in Melissa's locker, under the windshield of her Mustang. She goes to the ladies' room, and when she comes back there's one under her plate, another tucked in a napkin. Some are delivered by sled dog, others dropped by parachute, occasionally taped to a baffled hen. The post office delivers the others without even a street address because she's as famous as Santa. Melissa considers it her duty to read each one, but because she can't reply to all, she doesn't reply to any; Melissa does not play favorites. She does, however, really like the ones from children: "You are like the sun. Congratulations!" "If I was snow, I'd land on your head and melt." "When I cry, I think of you and feel better." And the unusual ones are interesting: "I would hold you for nothing in my arms." "Even if you didn't say anything, I would listen." "Those aren't the lights of the city, but the fireflies of my longing." There's even a kind of eloquence in the traditional: "My heart quickens every time I see you." "There's no one like you." "I'm too shy to say hello in person." Then one day she's reading love letters, and it occurs to her that others need them more than she: the boy shooting hoops by himself, the girl at Starbucks with a scar, the science teacher with his nine dogs—just the general loneliness and longing in almost everyone's eyes. Of course it means picking and choosing, sifting and sorting. "Whose woods these are, I think I know, but they're yours if you just say the word, baby." Nix on that one. But many will do. Most, actually. She scissors away the salutation and signature and secretly distributes the rest. Next day she notices the difference: a new dress, a clean shirt, some general buoyancy, the presence of shy smiles. For a while. But when there are no more letters, a new gloom descends. Worse than before. When it comes out that she is the culprit, that the compliments were meant for her, that

15

Melissa sees others as charity cases, she is reviled. Yelled at. Her mail turns hateful, her phone messages obscene.

"I only wanted to help," she cries.

"Oh please. How could you possibly understand!"

BEAUTY VOLUNTEERS

She signed up, so she went, driving her convertible over to Golden Acres. From the outside it's as advertised: Gilded in the sunlight. A mighty oak or two. There's an artist's rendition of a cozy apartment, complete with docile pet. Two painted seniors (not high school seniors but real ones) adorn the mural. He's robust with a five iron and Lacoste polo shirt. She's laughing gaily at a putter, her hair short enough for an active lifestyle, long enough not to suggest strange sexual preferences. Inside, it smells. Just a little. But it does smell. Like Lysol. And Simple Green. And other smells not from a bottle. Nurse Spud hands her a smock. With a stain. Melissa frowns. "I pictured something with stripes. Red and white stripes. Vertical ones to make me look even taller. But never mind." Nurse Spud, too tired to even look up: "Help me lift Mr. Dickens." Melissa gets both hands under those bony shoulders. His breath smells like yesterday. Melissa: "Goodness, he's awfully heavy. I imagined handing out magazines to brighten people's days." Nurse: "If you can't lift, get the bedpan from Room 209." Melissa: "Are there rubber gloves? I'm sure I need rubber gloves. In beige. Or may I just open the venetian blinds and let the sun in onto napping octogenarians in pressed pajamas?" Nurse: "Help me push this gurney." Melissa: "The big one? With that enormous person on it? Where is the retired CEO with just a slight fever who needs a cool cloth at his brow?" Nurse: "At least look in on Mrs. Rose." Who turns out to be thorny indeed: Her bedspread is too heavy, the TV too loud, the light too bright, magazines too depressing. And that hand! Wrinkled, gnarled, cold, human. OK, Melissa had been thinking about fitting in, being more like everyone else. But not so abruptly. Someday maybe. Not now. No wonder Melissa prefers the warm congratulations of the pageant judges. The limber fingers of those so glad to meet her. She returns to Nurse Spud: "How can you do this every day?" Nurse: "I've got a mortgage and car payments." She barely glances at Melissa. "You will too someday, cutie." Melissa bolts, leaving her smock on the floor by the puddle. The one Mr. Dickens made.

BEAUTY PASSES THE TEST

It's in Honors English, and nearly every question is about symbol and allegory. Melissa has this one aced. Not only does she always listen and take notes, she actually reads the books! So she knows *Pilgrim's Progress:* anxious Christian, the Valley of Humiliation, Doubting Castle. She's just finishing up when the door opens and in come all the answers on her exam, most wearing sandals and—as often as not—pale, with flowing robes. "Rise, Beauty," they chant, "and walk beside us." She's tentative at first, but soon smiles when Generosity hands her a hundred dollars, then joins Health for a chat about organic food. Although there aren't any cars, Safety cautions her to look both ways, then joins Virtue and begins to talk to a Health Ed. class. Beauty is enjoying herself. It's a pleasure to actually see Justice with her famous scales and blindfold being led about by Duty. Hilarity's high-pitched cackle and endless knee-slapping makes Optimism suggest, "Maybe tomorrow she'll put a lid on it." But there is always Peace and Quiet over by the stream, reading and eating grapes. Then something grotesque stumbles in late. Something damp and deformed, something misshapen and clumsy, ghastly and repulsive. Something, in short, ugly. In fact, Ugliness itself. Denial hurries by handing out those special glasses. Beauty reaches for a pair, but Ugliness slaps them away. "So proud of herself," Ugliness croaks. "But where would you be without me?" Beauty doesn't know what to say, but she does listen. "It's the dark that makes the light so inviting. The reason opposites attract is because they're essential to each other. What is Generosity without Selfishness? Without Practicality, Idealism gets nothing done." Beauty looks around. Sure enough, Innocence chats with Guilt on their way to court. Truth laughs at Falsehood's elaborate lies. Meaning sits down for coffee with Nonsense. Beauty looks at Ugliness. "So," she says, "without you, I wouldn't even exist?" Ugliness nods, grins horribly, and extends . . . something: part claw, part tentacle, part hand. And Beauty, to her undying credit, takes it.

FARANG

Mary Ann Rodman

Farang. My first Thai word. The word Kuhn Noi had taught me, the syllables floating light and flute-like.

This morning, in the school courtyard, *"farang"* sounds sharp and nasal in Nikki's Midwestern accent.

"It means 'foreigner,' "she says. "It means me and you and anybody else not Thai."

I knew what it meant, but the thought slams me like an algebra pop quiz. I'm not a foreigner.

But I am.

Dad's company has transferred him to Thailand.

So here I am. The foreigner. A *farang.*

I think about my friends, starting their sophomore year, too. A million miles away, back in Atlanta.

"Is Bangkok beautiful? Exotic?" they ask by e-mail.

"Yes. No." It is and it isn't. The images jump around in my head, like those old slides of Europe that my grandparents used to make me watch. Click. Here's Grandpa at the Eiffel Tower. Click. Here's Gramma in front of Big Ben.

With me, it's: Click. Temples, glittering with colored mirror tile. Click. Open sewers. Click. Orchids growing wild on tree trunks. Click. Packs of rabid dogs, wandering the streets.

"It's cool," I lie. It's too complicated to explain, especially on e-mail. E-mail, not IM, because you can't IM somebody who's twelve hours away, in another day of the week.

I don't feel cool at all, this morning, standing in the courtyard of the Bangkok American School, with Nikki, my principal-appointed "angel" this first day. Nikki's face has had the same expression since we met a half hour ago: pained boredom.

"Why don't you show Lauren around before the first bell?" the principal (whose name I've already forgotten) suggested.

Nikki dragged me through miles of empty hallways that all looked alike. After about ten minutes, she said, "OK, so, like, we aren't allowed in the building until first bell. Everybody hangs in the courtyard, if it isn't raining."

That's where we are now. In the courtyard, with about a thousand other kids, milling around. It could be any high school. It could be Atlanta.

"*Farang*," Nikki repeats. "Thais don't mix with *farangs*. They keep to themselves."

Nope, not Atlanta.

"They do?" I wave toward a knot of Thai girls in short denim skirts and high platforms. "Then why are they at the American School?"

"They want to go to college in the States." Nikki curls her lip. "Work for American companies. Marry American men."

Nikki's words march through my head, a straight line from high school to marriage. How can she see these things? I can't see past my first class this morning, which my schedule says is World Literature.

"Laura," says Angel Nikki, looking me up and down. Not in a friendly way.

"It's Lauren," I say.

"Sorry, Lauren." Nikki's voice says, "Whatever." "Where do you shop?"

I name a mall store in Atlanta. Wrong answer.

"Everybody here wears Gap," she says.

"Oh. OK. So I'll go to the Gap."

"*Farangs* can't buy off the rack." Nikki smiles. A nasty smile. "The clothes are made for the locals. And they're all about the size of my little brother. He's ten."

She has a point. The Thai girls high-step by us in their platforms. The shoes make them look tall and storklike, but their bodies are tiny, tiny. Less-than-zero tiny.

I shrug. "So, I can order online."

Nikki shakes her head. "You can't. The custom taxes are more than what you pay for the clothes." She looks pleased to be delivering bad news.

"So where do you buy clothes?" I ask.

"In the States. On furlough." Nikki flickers her fingers as if to say, "Duh, of course."

We won't get furlough until Christmas. I shrink a little more into my "wrong" clothes.

A bell shrills. Nikki and I plunge into a swirling mass of kids shoving their way into the building at the first bell.

I am invisible.

There are invisible kids in every school. Not nerds or misfits or obvious freaks. Just anonymous. The ones in the yearbook I swear I've never seen before. Kids who fade into the walls.

Gap-dressed kids stream by me, pressing me against the wall. My pale, pinky-white skin matches the wall color perfectly. Lauren, the Amazing Wall-Colored Girl!

Nikki dumps me off at World Lit.

"I'll find you for lunch," she says. It sounds like a threat.

At lunchtime, Nikki and I wedge into the food line. I scan the cafeteria. I am the only person my color.

Oh, there are plenty of Caucasians. The ones with permanent perfect tans. The ones Mom predicts will "look like shoe leather when they're forty." Well, maybe, but right now they look hot. Who cares about forty?

They have perfect tans and teeth and everything else. It's like being in the middle of a TV movie about high school, where everybody is supposed to be sixteen, but you know the actors are really thirty. Perfect hair, perfect teeth. Perfect outfits.

The Thai girls especially. Like they're trying to blend in. Look American. Which is weird because all the Thai girls are incredibly gorgeous with honey-colored skin and silky waterfalls of hair.

We move up to the steam tables. "You can get Thai, American, or vegetarian," Nikki yells over clattering trays and four hundred kids talking. I look at the glistening piles of unfamiliar foods. At home, Kuhn Noi makes familiar American food.

"Hurry up," Nikki snaps. "We only have twenty minutes."

I quickly point to the only familiar items in the

line, a burger and fries. Nikki and I elbow our way to a table of Perfect American Teens, all named Megan or Christopher.

"So where are you from?" a blond Megan asks me.

"Atlanta." My fries taste weird.

"I mean overseas." The Megan pokes at a plate of Thai noodles. She looks more interested in rearranging her lunch.

"I've never lived overseas before." Peanut oil. The fries were cooked in peanut oil. And the burger is seasoned with lemongrass. The "American" lunch is a big mistake.

"Oh." The Megan divides her noodles into little piles. End of conversation.

The Megans and Christophers are more than happy to tell me where they've lived. Seoul. Sydney. Singapore. None of them has spent much time in the States. They all call it "home," but they've never lived there.

They don't really have a home.

It's a scary thought.

Almost as scary as the rest of the conversation. Lunch reminds me of a TV show I saw back in

Atlanta. It was about something called "speed dating." These single people would get together and talk
one-on-one for five minutes. Then a timer would go
off. Everybody would change partners and talk to
somebody else for five minutes. At the end of the
evening, they would ask out the people who had been
interesting for five minutes.

The Megans and Christophers ask all these questions. A wrong answer, and I'm history.

"Hey, wait a minute!" I want to yell. "Give me a
chance." But the questions keep coming. This *is* the
chance.

I see them taking me in. All of me. No-color hair,
nothing sort of face, the wrong clothes. Not fat, not
thin. Not short, not tall.

Just not.

Suddenly, like someone has turned off a switch,
the questions stop.

And the ignoring starts. Conversation shoots over
and around me.

I'm out.

"Did you hear what happened to Jordan?" asks a

Christopher with spiky blond hair. "Moved to Beijing over the weekend. Didn't even get to say bye."

"Bummer," says another Christopher through a mouthful of fries.

Then I get it. In this world, transfers can happen over the weekend. People decide who you are in a twenty-minute lunch.

I am doomed.

When I come home from school, Kuhn Noi is in the kitchen, chopping mangoes for a fruit salad.

"*Sawasdee ka,* Kuhn Lauren," she says. "*Sawasdee*" is an all-purpose greeting, just as "Kuhn" is a title of respect tacked on before names.

Kuhn Noi hands me a piece of mango.

"*Kop juhn ka,*" I say. "Thank you," "hello," and "foreigner" are my entire Thai vocabulary.

I suck the juice from the mango as I watch Kuhn Noi's knife flash in the afternoon sunlight.

I think about how Mom freaked when she learned that not only were we getting a housekeeper, but that she would live in the maid's room behind the kitchen.

29

"I can do my own housekeeping, thank you," Mom insisted. "I don't want some strange woman living in my apartment."

"Most Thais don't speak English," said Dad. "And Thai is almost impossible for an adult to learn. You will need someone to grocery shop for you."

"I can't buy my own food?" Mom looked at Dad like he'd lost his mind.

"Produce is bought from the street market. And even if you could speak Thai well enough to haggle, the vendors tend to have two prices. One for Thais and one for foreigners."

So Kuhn Noi, a little walnut of a woman, who could be any age between twenty and death, came to live in the closet behind the kitchen. Only her eyes tell me that she is far older than she looks. Her eyes glow like the burnished mahogany walls of the apartment. Wise, ancient eyes.

Kuhn Noi is my best friend.

"More mango?" asks Kuhn Noi. I take another sliver from her elegant brown fingers.

According to other *farangs,* you should not be friendly with "the servants."

"They won't respect you," the *farangs* say. "They will take advantage."

But Kuhn Noi isn't like that. For one thing, she is much older than the hill country nannies I see at the pool or park. They are sturdy and round faced, with long braids and gap-toothed smiles, and they don't speak English.

Kuhn Noi is small, birdlike, and hides her hair under a silk scarf wound around her head. She also speaks excellent English.

"I work for many American," she tells me. "They teach me English. Americans have good heart."

For Kuhn Noi, everyone has either a bad heart or a good heart.

The kitchen is the center of Kuhn Noi's world. After homework and supper, I go there to talk to her. When the dishes are done and the countertops clean, this is the maid's living room. Sometimes, late at night, I hear the high-pitched chatter of other maids.

"We talk about our madams," says Kuhn Noi when I ask. The maids call their female employers "madam."

Kuhn Noi files her tiny almond-shaped nails. Her hands are wrinkled and rough from endless hot-water scrubbings of floors and windows and dishes. But that doesn't stop her nightly manicure.

"Prani, from fourth floor, she quit her madam. She go home to vote and not come back."

"Why?" I ask.

"Her madam fat. She lose face working for a fat woman."

For a minute, I think Kuhn Noi is kidding. But Thais do not make that kind of joke. I know Prani's madam. She's a little big in the butt, but she sure isn't fat.

"The maids, they say, 'Noi, you work for fat woman.'" Kuhn Noi carefully brushes on clear nail polish.

I listen, fascinated. Horrified. Is this how the Thais see us? Mom is no hot babe, but she's not supposed to be. She's a mom!

"But I say, 'Yes, madam fat. But she has whitest

skin in whole building.' " Kuhn Noi splays her newly
polished fingers on a worn-out towel to dry. " 'And a
good heart, too.' "

I look down at my own not-so-skinny white arms.
Kuhn Noi catches me.

"You have pretty white skin, like madam. You take
care. No go out in sun without sunblock. You no
want to be like Kuhn Noi." She reaches into her flow-
ered silk makeup bag and pulls out a blue plastic jar
with fancy gold Thai script on the label. A very
white-skinned Thai woman in a slinky dress lounges
across the lettering.

"What's that?" I ask as Kuhn Noi dips the ends of
her fingers into the pink stuff and rubs it into the
backs of her hands.

"Bleach cream." She slathers it from wrist to elbow
and massages it in. "White skin, very beautiful." She
starts on her face.

Back in Atlanta, the drugstores sold bleach creams,
too. Only the women on those jars were light-skinned
black women. I always thought it was pathetic that
someone would want to change their skin color.

I decide that Kuhn Noi only wants to turn her skin to the buttercream color of my Thai classmates. I can understand that. I'd like to be a slightly different color myself. Only darker.

Still, it's sad. After all, Kuhn Noi has a "good heart." But good hearts don't show the way that light skin and long shiny hair do.

Another day, another lunch with the Megans. No one speaks to me. I am invisible. The Megans talk about plastic surgery.

"It is sooo cheap here," says a long-haired Megan. "Mama absolutely promised I could have my nose done during winter break."

Why? Her nose looks fine to me.

"Well, don't go to that doctor Ashley went to," says Nikki. "She looks totally worse."

"What Ashley needs is a head transplant," says the Megan.

They all laugh. I take my tray to the garbage chute. Another burst of laughter as I pass the table. What are the Megans saying about me?

I have ten minutes before class. In the restroom, I hear the same sounds I heard in the bathroom of my old school after lunch. Girls throwing up. Cough. Gag. Spit. Flush. It sounds like every stall has a girl with a finger down her throat.

I am scared in this country. Not of the country. But of the *farangs*.

I try to find a place at the mirror, but I have to wait. Girls lip-glossing, hair-brushing, or just looking. Looking for what? What do they see?

Finally, it's my turn at the mirror.

Next to me, a Thai girl tosses a pouch purse the size of a laundry bag onto the narrow shelf beneath the mirror. Someone calls to her in Thai. She turns quickly, knocking her purse to the floor with a crunchy whack. Pens and combs and lip gloss roll from the purse's mouth.

And a jar. A blue plastic jar with a white-skinned Thai babe on the label. The jar lands at my feet.

Kuhn Noi's jar.

The slide show runs in my head. A foreign land.

Click. American girls, throwing up. Click. Thai girls, dressed like American girls. Click. A woman with a good heart. Click. A jar of bleach cream.

I hand the girl the jar.

"*Kop juhn ka,*" she mumbles, but her eyes are sad and envious. Of me.

The girl with the wall-colored skin.

I am sad too, for this girl—this girl with honey skin and silky hair and graceful hands.

Here in the land of beauty, we are all *farangs.*

Rover, Rover

Chris Lynch

I never loved anybody, before a Saturday in June. Actually it would have been Sunday, since all the stuff that happened happened mostly after the dateline, after midnight, which I figure is when most of the real things in life happen. I usually sleep through them.

Love, though. Never really, anyway, love. As far as I know. As far as I can tell, I never loved anybody, except for possibly my mother, before Saturday. Or Sunday. It wasn't by choice. Not a decision I made, or something I controlled. It was just not what I did with people. With people? To people? At them, around them? What is it you do with love, anyway? Not important. The thing is, it was just not my thing, and it was not my fault. It just was.

"Well, certainly, it's hot. Sure, it's hot. We all feel the heat, and we're free to move around. We are free to go outside, and to have a smoke, and to drink a couple of icy-cold Diet Cokes, if we so desire. For you, in this . . . *thing,* god, it has to be ten times worse with the heat."

It, this *thing,* would be my bed. The Stryker bed.

Sounds dynamic, no?

No.

Here's what the Stryker bed does. It makes a sandwich out of you, and then it makes a rotisserie chicken out of you, and if I'm leaning a little heavy on the food comparisons, then that's fair enough because the other thing the Stryker bed does to me is it makes me want to tell everybody to just *eat me.*

Sorry. But what it is, it's like a cot type of bed and every two hours when I'll be just lying on my back—

you know my back, the broken one—being a brave young soldier indeed, the team comes in and clamps a whole other cot right down on top of me. There's a little hole cut for my face so I can do things like see and breathe and probably I look like the carnival attraction where you try to bop the clown with a baseball. Maybe we'll play it, eventually.

There's no need for more entertainment yet, though, because the best part is next. That's when my handlers all get together and heave-ho, here we go. They crank a handle and shove me over until the world does a quick gainer with a half twist and I come to a stop with a thump that leaves my spine feeling like it's tearing off in two directions. I'm staring at the speckled, screaming-white tiled floor through my Stryker cot face-hole, adding more screaming and speckling to the floor because I am crying my guts out all over it.

Every two hours, pretty much the same scene.

I am very sorry about that. Because I know what I look like when I cry. That is why I stopped crying when I was five. Caught a glimpse of my yogurt cheeks, my brown-spotted forehead, my copper-wiring hair matting down along throbbing, veiny temples, and I scared myself completely and permanently straight. I looked like Raggedy Ann, if she were sitting on the tip of a flaming spear. So the crying thing just couldn't happen.

And didn't. For twelve tight-ass years. Until a Saturday in June. Sunday.

Here's what I did, on Saturday night. It is a thing I do. Not the breaking-my-back thing, which was kind of a special-occasion deal, but the rest of it. I drive out almost every Saturday night unless I have another engagement—which is another way of saying I drive out every Saturday night—to the airport.

I don't have any business there, I just go. I do like other people; I watch planes take off and land, I have something to eat. I try to get around to all the different restaurants in all the different terminals, for variety, and have a little meal there. I'm compiling a little book of reviews that I'm clipping together for I'm not sure what. Maybe somebody will like it. Maybe it will be useful sometime even though the restaurants all look and taste the same.

After I eat, I walk, because that is good for digestion. It is also good for looking at people. I stare at people. I try not to stare, but I know I am doing it because of the bug-eyed, mind-your-business look I get when I am caught. I don't stop, though. I watch all the couples and the families and the rowdy-guys groups. I like to watch especially at the big airport moments, when lots of people are just slamming back together after somebody's trip, and lots more are yanking apart because the airline is making them say good-bye *right this minute*. Airports are all about tears and giggles, and you really can't help but feel somehow like you are part of it, especially if you go regularly like I do and so are a natural part of the scenery.

Sometimes I go to a greeting area, like outside of customs at the international terminal, and I wait there for a long time, just as if I were there to pick somebody up. But toward the end, when most people have been picked up, the only ones left are the raggedy stragglers who look half dead and wholly alone because nobody is there for them. When they come, I go, because they kind of spoil it.

But none of all this broke my back, did it? No, what broke my back was that I was driving way too fast, far too fast, late Saturday night to get away from that airport. I don't drive fast; I know better. I stopped driving fast when earlier in the year, at the start of my senior year, our headmaster addressed us all in the auditorium, pointed his finger out over the crowd, and insisted, "Two to four of you people will not be here for graduation. That is what happens every year. And we will probably lose you in an automobile. Try and make it to graduation, kids." And that was it; he left the stage.

Pretty effective speech, as far as these things go. It worked on me, anyway. I wanted to live, and I wanted to graduate. Not entirely sure why, but there I was.

And I was a safe driver before a Saturday night in June. Before I felt a need to speed away from the airport and flew through the airport tunnel probably faster than the planes above it, and flew out of the tunnel far too fast for anybody who seriously wanted to make the sharp right turn up the upramp to the expressway.

And so, violence. I have millions of flaws, more flaws than almost anybody, more flaws on my anemic face alone than you probably have in your whole soul. Except that the main flaw I always did not have was violence. I was never in any way a violent guy, and never once did I deliberately hurt another body's outsides.

But now it comes in bunches. Day and night, but especially night, the violence, the visions, the scenes come in monster waves. Me fighting. Me driving fast, faster, aiming for a crash. Blood, and speed, and shattering bones, and stuff that before a Saturday night in June was never, ever a part of my life is suddenly very central to my nightly life. In nearly every scene, my skull winds up mashed like rotten fruit.

Morphine, I think, has something to do with it. They give me, apparently, as much as they are allowed, because I am broken pretty good, and my

43

genius surgeon who is busy but worth the wait is keeping me waiting, keeping me broken, for a week before operating. It kind of hurts a lot when we are nearing time for my next morphine. But then, right after, other things take over.

"You know, Nursey-Nurse, I'm one of those guys who lives life too close to the edge. That's what got me in this situation."

"No, I think it's riding too close to the guardrail that got you in this situation."

I hate that she is funny. I especially hate that she is funnier than me.

"Are you a redhead?" I say. "God, I would just hate it if you were a redhead. That's the only thing, if you were a redhead. We can get along fine no matter what other problems you have."

My nickname my entire school life was Red Rover. Or, if they had a little extra time, Red Rover, Red Rover. Or, if things were especially slow, Red Rover, Red Rover, Send Ass-Face Right Over. And so on. But I'm not in school anymore. I just graduated.

"Because. You see, my mother was a redhead. I

could kill her. No, she is alive. I could kill her, though. Red. She's red. And I will never forgive her for that. And even now, when it's fading and her hair is turning an almost-hair-color-normal-for-humans, what do you suppose she does? She gets some stuff and she starts *dyeing* it back. After she's recovered. After she's been cured, she starts giving herself the disease again. I mean, could you kill her? I could kill her. I love her, but I could kill her. You're not a red-head, are you, Nursey-Nurse?"

"I am not *Nursey-Nurse,* thank you." You had to hear the perfect note on the second *nurse.* Banged it like a gong. Hilarious. Very good, very funny, like a pro. I hate it. "You can call me Nurse Knightly, like I told you before."

Nurse Knightly is doing stuff behind me, what stuff I have no idea. That is how it is every time because Nurse Knightly only ever shows up in the middle of the night and only after I have been spun over onto my face. We have met several times, but we've never actually seen each other. Nurse Knightly is a presence; a pair of busy, efficient, strong-gentle hands; and a voice. A deep, rich, sure voice. Deeper than mine, higher than my mother's. That is all I know of my midnight nurse, and I keep it this way by keeping my face pressed firmly toward the floor. I could see with mirrors. They said I can have mirrors if I want. I don't want.

"Nurse Knightly," I say in a very nice, obedient, schoolboy voice, "are you a guy or a gal?"

There's a snort, a bull snort that shoots in my direction. I may even hear a hoof pawing the floor.

"I am *not* a gal."

"Hah! I knew I—"

"I am not a *gal,* because nobody is a *gal* in this universe, in this century, you sad little cowboy."

I laugh, but mostly on the inside. Laughing on the outside hurts my spine so much that I have to distribute my laughter evenly in a smooth howl-growl dial-tone noise that really cracks up Nurse Knightly, which then gets me going and I wind up killing myself with the hard, choppy guffaws I was trying to avoid in the first place.

"Shall I rephrase the question, then?" I ask chirpily.

This is not the first phrasing of this question between us, actually. And they have all been just this fun for me.

"You can rephrase it into Serbo-Croatian if you like, but you'll get the same nothing out of me."

I love Nurse Knightly.

"I love you, Nurse Knightly." Damn-god-damn I cannot believe I let that out. Fortunately, Nurse Knightly knows me intimately and reorders things.

"Hmm, you may love me, but I suspect you love morphine just a little bit more."

"It is so hot." I moan almost involuntarily because it hits me now just how stifling they keep a hospital room that should be making the likes of me a little more comfortable.

"I know," says Nurse Knightly calmly.

They wake me up every couple of hours no matter what, to make sure I keep. Healthy. No skin sores and all that, keep my blood moving around my body and all. And keep that stupid spine and all its horrible little splinters locked in place until genius surgeon, who is also very tall and not redheaded and probably has his own airplane, can get in there and stick in the steel rods that will make me more rigid than the wet stick of gum that I am now. I know all the why of why they have to do it. But hell. Hell. I'd have rather just stayed asleep, if anybody asked me. I'd have taken the sores, and the risks, actually, if anybody asked me.

But nobody asked me.

Except.

"What can I do for you to make you feel better?" is what I hear, every night, at about zero in the morning, when I am lying facedown, in the Stryker bed, in some discomfort, and when I can see not one sign of life.

At first I could not believe this was legitimate. I thought it had to be a gag. A rotten gag.

"What can you *do* for me? Are you joking?"

"No. I'm not joking, actually. Are you feeling all right? That is my purpose, after all, to help you feel better. Call it job satisfaction, I guess. But it does matter to me whether or not you feel better. If you don't, I'll go home and feel terrible for the rest of the night. I mean that. That's the way I am."

"Get out of town, because that is *not* the way you

are. That's not the way anybody is. Nobody is that good. Sorry."

"No, don't be sorry. You're right, nobody is that good. But for now, would you like me to give you a little alcohol rub, which will help you feel cooler and a lot more comfortable?"

It is more than fair to say that I've had very little experience with fielding an offer like that. But even instincts as miserable as mine say not to go all quivery with excitement.

"Um, sure, I guess you could do that."

"Great. It's a date."

A date. Yikes, a date.

"Yikes, a date."

Nurse Knightly laughs—a barrelly, rugged, knee-slapper laugh.

"You are so funny. I didn't think anybody really said 'yikes.' But there you go."

"There I go. But I didn't mean to go there. I wasn't supposed to say the 'yikes, a date' thing for you to hear it. Wasn't even entirely sure I did, until right there when you told me and laughed at me."

"Oh gee, I didn't laugh *at* you, like that. I'm sorry—"

"Don't be sorry. In fact, if you'll laugh just that way once more, I'll say it all over again."

I don't even have to say it over again.

"That's a great laugh, you know. Makes a guy want to be funny just to hear it."

"Well, there you go. Everybody wins."

I certainly do. Nurse Knightly proceeds to politely undo the back of my humiliating hospital-boy outfit, then spritzes the finest mist of alcohol across my shoulder blades, carefully out to my sides, moving down but staying safely away from the spine. Then, the spine.

I could holler with joy, if I could even talk. I could not have guessed this feeling of relief, of coolness, yes, but more of total tingly bliss, as the alcohol touches me all over my back, all over where nothing and nobody has been able to touch me since a June Saturday night or Sunday. Then, with careful fingers, applied just barely heavier than the alcohol mist, Nurse Knightly rubs and feather-strokes my sides, my shoulder blades, my neck, and I don't know if it is the alcohol or the application of it, but I swear I can feel it seeping under the skin, into my body, cooling my surface and setting fire to my insides.

I close my eyes. I squeeze them extra-tight because inexplicably, like an imbecile, I am about to cry again. If I do, I swear I will slap myself. There is no pain here, so there is no excuse here. I can cry in another hour, when they flip me over, but not now. I'm going to blow the whole thing, and Nurse Knightly will stop rubbing me and then never show up in my room again, I just know it.

"How is that, then? Is that all right? You feeling any better?"

I am not sure if a sound comes out of me. I can only hope it was yes-like.

So I haven't blown it anyway. In fact, it gets better. Nurse Knightly leans over a bit closer. I can feel features there, can almost feel nose and lips against my back, at the most dangerous, do-not-touch, shattered area of my middle spine. And then, just then, just so, Nurse Knightly's breath goes where the fingers cannot, a swinging, slow, side-to-side, then up-and-down motion, as if a team of little wings are aligned for the sole purpose of making me feel better.

And that is just what they do, and just what I feel. Better. Better than before. Better than you. Better than anyone anywhere at this moment. My back may have even healed, I feel so much better. So much better, I suddenly panic, afraid that I am going to embarrass myself. I feel myself breathing faster, in those safe, shallow breaths they taught me so I wouldn't get any more hurt.

Nurse Knightly is perfect.

We have a silence now that I am too aware of. We don't have silences much once we get going, me and Nurse Knightly, and I don't like them when we do. They are big, fat blobs in the middle of our fine, clean space, and I don't like them at all. My back rub has ended, and I need to say something about it. I have to, I should, I want to. I want to say it all, and I will never be able to say enough.

But sometimes I think, and nothing comes out. I realize it's more the morphine, but it's a terror anyway, like I'm in a trap in my own head.

God, how I do wish that silence would shut up now. It is a fright to me.

Nurse Knightly must have hit a glitch too, because this should have stopped already. And when finally it does, it's as if the conversation has skipped backward.

" 'Yikes, a date,' you say?"

I am politely rebuttoned. My nurse is up and about the room again doing stuff. Rubbing alcohol is now my favorite scent.

"Argh," I say.

The laugh. Throaty. Meaty. "You also say 'argh'? Where did you go to school, Marvel Comics?"

"Listen, pretend I didn't say 'yikes, a date.' It was the morphine talking."

"OK, I'll try and pretend. But don't get your hopes up."

Again the blob of silence descends, and again I hate it. But this time the morphine does its other trick, ending the silence. Go, Morph.

"Yikes, it was the morphine talking. Want to hear it talk again?"

God, no. I can almost actually hear this inside, the good region of my mind cringing and begging the other part to stop.

"OK, here goes." It's not listening to anyone now. "I want you to know that that back rub was the finest thing that ever happened to me. The best moment of my life."

I think I registered with that one.

"Whoa!"

"And hear that? Now I know who it is. Lucille Ball. There was a show, back in the Stone Age, probably the first television show, *I Love Lucy.* And my mother used to force everybody to watch it whenever it was on. You would have to sit there right in front of the TV like a zombie, like a cult brainwashing indoctrination. My mother always loved her. Lucy was a mad redhead, you see. Even though she was in black and white, she wasn't fooling anybody. We could tell."

I believe I have Nurse Knightly pretty well spell-bound by now.

"I am familiar with Lucy. Is there a reason why we're talking about her?"

"Oh. Sorry, it's the voice. That's who your voice sounds like. She had a deep, unusual voice. And especially later, when she had another show—in color, unfortunately—and she was older and had smoked millions more cigarettes that made it even deeper . . . that, right there, is the voice."

There is a bit of a pause where I find myself weirdly sort of congratulating myself for something here. I don't know what I thought this Lucy connection would mean. People can be funny sometimes, about being compared.

"Thanks," Nurse Knightly says in exactly that voice. Amazing, really.

"My mother would love you," I say. "She would really love you, my mother."

That one just stays there in the air, uncollected, as I hear Nurse Knightly clanking things and clicking things and doing the nurse job just for me. I think I need to say thank you for that, and it is on my lips when I hear my nurse swoosh out the door.

To go and do it for somebody else, I suppose. I suppose that's only fair. I suppose that is the way it has to work, and that I knew that.

When my nurse returns some time later—minutes probably, but it passed like a whole lonely summer—I am twitching with more pain and discomfort than if it was my morphine running late.

"I haven't had very many dates," I say.

"'Scuse? Were you talking all the time I was out of the room and now I'm off the pace?"

"No, it's me. The 'yikes' thing. 'Yikes, a date,' remember? I thought I would, sort of, explain that now. I have had very few dates."

"I find that strange and nearly impossible to believe."

"No, you don't, but thank you. The front of my head is even more a mess than the back. The front has got *details*."

"I won't listen anymore if it's going to go like this."

"And of those pathetic few dates, almost all of

them were with this girl named Cherry, who was right up my alley because she had a face like a shoe and was homeschooled her entire life all the way until she was sixteen and her parents split up spectacularly and there was no home to be schooled in anymore. So Cherry was plopped like a six-foot-tall infant into the middle of our junior year of high school with absolutely nothing for social skills and, as I said, a face like a shoe.

"*And,* get ready now, even with all that going for her, the first *seven* times I asked her out she said *no!*"

"Ah, but you stuck with it, and the important thing is you won her over in the end. Lucky number eight."

"Lucky nothing, she thought I was somebody else. I eventually wrote her a note, signed it from the *second* ugliest guy in the school, and she jumped at it like a marlin. I asked her to meet me at this Chinese restaurant near the school, not the greatest Chinese restaurant but just within my budget and quality requirements, because I was going to do it right and pay for everything and encourage her to get more than she wanted and dessert and everything. And thanks only to her *E. T.*-level of social experience did she not think this was a setup. Cherry actually came to the restaurant expecting a romantic date rather than, say, a bunch of seniors jumping out from behind the hundred-gallon fish tank to pelt her with wontons until she cried and capturing it all on film. I would have expected something like that. I think most normal people who knew some things and had met the world before would have expected something was up. Not Cherry. Only Cherry. Very Cherry.

"But what she got was me. She may not have considered that a brilliant consolation, but we did get together. She saw me there, looked around hopefully for a better explanation, then figured it out after a few minutes. Then she sighed in a very tired way and spoke those romantic words which will live in my heart forever: 'I suppose.'

"I was kind of scared and depressed from that very first minute we got together, and she looked like she felt exactly the same. She looked tired when I felt tired. She looked suicidal when I felt suicidal.

It was less like two people and more like one monkey not understanding his reflection in a mirror. Eventually I realized that I had put all this effort into dating . . . myself. And I had hoped to do better than that. We were different enough, but really, we were the same. You could rearrange our features and trade them around like Mr. and Mrs. Potato Head, but still, in there, we would see each other. It made me angry when I would see myself in there. Angrier every time.

"And I felt sorry. For her. 'Cause you know what? I really liked her. And you know what? In those moments when I could stop seeing me where she was supposed to be? Cherry was really pretty. Even though her face was shaped just a little like the sole of a shoe, it didn't spoil it. It suited her.

"Until I saw me there again, and not her.

"By the time we did actually manage to have sex, which we managed exactly two times, it was more like a dare than anything else. A challenge, a joust. A punishment. We probably didn't do it any worse than most people do the first times. But it was worse, because *we* were there. And we would not let each other forget that.

"Want to hear it some more, Nurse Knightly? Ready to hear more from Morph?"

She blobs me with more silence. She knows what she is doing, but it will not work.

"Here it is, then. You know how I got through sex with Cherry? Both times? I fantasized of course. What did I fantasize about? I fantasized about masturbating. What do you think, Nurse? As a professional human bodyist, do you think I might have the arrangement a little backwards?"

"I am not an expert in the field, I'm afraid."

"Well, I am, now. I found it very relaxing. Because then I stopped feeling like I had to apologize to anybody else. Worked like a charm."

"Are you trying to scare me away now? Do I really sound easy to scare to you? You could just ask me to go, if you wanted me to go."

"And now, when I masturbate, want to know what I fantasize about? Go ahead, guess."

"No, thank you."

"When I masturbate, I fantasize about—ta-da—masturbating. The circle is finally unbroken. Neat little system, huh? Perfection."

"My shift is ending."

I know when shifts are ending, because I have gotten good at that, a sense of things, of time, of coming and going, that I didn't used to have. I am thinking about possibly asking Nurse Knightly to hold on just a few minutes for my next rotation so I can finally get a look as he or she leaves and doesn't ever come back. It is up to me, I know. I don't know.

I really did love my airport trip. I loved it a lot, and thought about it all week until the day. Now I can't even go. And I would be dressed nice, too, in very nice clothes like there was always something special on. Everybody in the airport is so beautiful. Everyone. Isn't that amazing?

Well, that time I went, one Saturday night in June, I had no idea I would see Cherry and her mother and father.

No idea I would ever see them together again *anywhere,* never mind at the airport. Which is why the sure and bitter taste of unrightness came up on me so fast, right when I saw them. You know when you just know? Especially when you so wish you didn't?

Can I say that of a whole airport full of pretty people, Cherry was the prettiest thing? Can I tell you she looked more lovely than the entire place? Lovelier than ten terminals put together. They all did, the reunited family—looked sparkling, as they stood in line getting ready to fly into some fresh, spotless new everything.

That's the airport for you, isn't it?

They didn't see me, of course, which was why Cherry didn't wave good-bye to me. It's one thing to pretend strangers are really your friends or family or lovers, but to intrude on real people you actually do know, the moment they're starting over again, that just wouldn't be right. So I just went away very, very quickly so as not to disturb or upset anybody.

I'm not telling the truth, completely.

I upset myself when I went away from that airport very, very quickly. I upset myself a whole lot, because I really did want for Cherry to see me there in the airport, in my airport look. I was dressed awfully nice. I did a good job getting ready that Saturday night in June. Cherry would have liked how I looked when I was in the airport, in my duds, in my airport mood.

I should have let her see me.

"Would you like me to stay with you for a while longer?" Nurse Knightly asks in an unnecessary whisper that makes me worry about myself. "I don't mind a bit."

"Were you reading my mind?"

"Good nurses can do that."

"I don't think I would recommend any more of it."

"Can't be any worse than what you actually say out loud."

"I apologize, Nurse, for attempting to be grotesque to you."

"Very good. So, I'll stay for a while."

"No."

"What? You don't want me?"

"Don't tease, please. You are dealing with an invalid, you know. Of course I want you. But I don't mind you leaving. As long as I feel sure you're coming *back*."

"Sure, I am coming back. As long as you don't talk dirty anymore."

"OK. But can I make you my fantasy?"

I can hear Nurse Knightly sliding away as the team shuffles in to turn me over and make me cry. She stops in the doorway.

"I believe you may have mentioned you already had one."

"I would very much like to replace it with something nicer."

Words fight over a straining low laugh. "You going to need to have a look at me, then, to make this thing work?"

"Absolutely not. Absolutely no. Anyhow, I've got you already."

Nurse opens the door to my room once more just as the team is snapping the Stryker bed tightly over me and the checklist starts. Clip number three, tight, four locked . . .

"So," Nurse asks with a big, thick Lucy laugh, "how am I?"

I want to make a joke.

I want to make several.

But I have another glitch moment, and only real stuff comes out.

"Nurse, you are so beautiful, I'm blinded. You are the most gorgeous thing I have ever never seen."

The door to the room has already closed, but there is no missing the big voice bouncing around the corridor.

"Ha," says Nurse, "you must have been sneaking peeks all along."

I start laughing the wrong way, and it hurts like mad. The team jerks me over at just that moment, slams me to an awkward, excruciating stop, and the pain is immense.

But this time, I do not cry.

That's a lie. I cry like a brat.

But it's OK. It's only pain. And soon I am moaning a small, safe laugh. Right, then I'm crying again.

But after a while everything settles down. It's quiet, and I can lie back and think about truly lovely things.

Like being able to walk again.

Bad Hair Day

Lauren Myracle

"This is a complete and utter disaster," I pronounced.

"Zelly, please," Kristin said. Her tone was *Here we go again, Zelly being overdramatic.* "A disaster would be being attacked by a pit bull. A disaster would be a tidal wave, or being sold as a sex slave in the Philippines."

"Or having a hair sprout from your chin on the day you're supposed to be crowned Homecoming Queen," I said. "In five hours, Kris! Five hours until the stadium lights shine on me, me, me—*and my chin hair!*"

I could hear how self-absorbed I sounded, and I tried to get a grip. I did tend to be a little vain sometimes. I knew that. It was one of my flaws, along with . . . well, a lot of things. I had a lot of flaws! I admitted it! And one day I'd, you know, go live in a yurt and drink nothing but barley water until I achieved enlightenment. But not today. Not on Homecoming.

"Be honest," I said to Kristin. "Which would you rather have: tidal wave or chin hair?"

"Huh, think I'd take the chin hair."

"Well, *huh,* I think you wouldn't."

"Huh, I think you're freaking."

I glared. "Could we stop with the 'huh's?"

"Huh. Can we?"

I made an *aaargh* sound and closed my eyes. When I opened them, she was still there. So was my chin hair. It was black and wiry, gleaming in the girls' bathroom mirror.

"Just pluck it, will you?" I said. "It's mocking me."

"It's *mocking* you? How is it mocking you?"

"Well, look at it!"

We leaned toward the mirror. Kristin scrunched her eyes.

"Do you see?"

"It's tiny," she said. "It's cute."

"Kristin!"

Even though I knew she was kidding, there was a part of me that wondered if she was secretly delighted. Was she jealous that I was Homecoming Queen, even though she swore up and down she wasn't?

Don't hate me because I'm beautiful, I wanted to tell her.

The thing to remember was that I didn't ask to be Homecoming Queen. The football players voted, which, OK, was sexist and a little pervy, but tell that to the school administrators. The football players picked me, which was their way of saying I was the hottest girl in the class. What was I supposed to do? Decline? Renounce the throne to Scout Hopkins, who had the second most votes?

Scout Hopkins had something wrong with her. She never passed judgment on anyone, even famous people like Lindsay Lohan who would neither know nor care. Instead she said things like "She doesn't look fat; she looks happy," because that was the way of the Lord. Once I gave her a ride because her pickup broke down, and she tuned my radio to Wave, the Christian rock station. I so wanted Kristin there to laugh at it with. Although the music wasn't terrible. It was alarmingly catchy.

I very, very privately admired Scout for being such a good person, but I wasn't about to hand her my crown. The girl had stubby eyelashes, for heaven's sake. And she wore rodeo jeans. With tube socks.

I passed Kristin the tweezers from my contraband Swiss Army knife, which had my name in cursive swirled across the red casing. *Zelly,* with the "Z" all looped and sassy.

"My grammy has a chin hair," Kristin said. She squeezed the tweezers open and shut, like a tiny mouth. "More like a beard, really. I guess there's no one at the nursing home to pluck it for her."

"Get on with it," I said. Our free period would end within minutes, and girls would come streaming into the bathroom. Girls who were unhairy.

"Wouldn't that suck, to live in a nursing home and be covered in facial hair?" Kristin asked. "And moles. My grammy has a gazillion moles."

"I'd really appreciate it if we could stop with the chatter."

Kristin extended the tweezers. "On the count of three," she said. "One, two . . . three!"

"Ow!" I yelped.

Kristin examined the nose of the tweezers. "Sorry, didn't get it."

"That really hurt!"

"Let me try again. One, two . . . three!"

"*Ow!*"

She peered at my chin. "Oops."

"Kristin!"

"One more time—let me try one more time."

She grasped the hair, and I squeezed shut my eyes. She gave a mighty yank.

"*OW!*" I howled. "Owie owie ow!"

"It's very resistant!" Kristin cried. "I don't think it *wants* to come out!"

"You're fired," I said, snatching the tweezers.

The bell rang. A posse of volleyball players swarmed into the bathroom, and I tucked my chin.

"Does anyone have a brush?" a girl named Solange asked. She jostled for a place at the mirror as mascara wands were whipped out and lipsticks uncapped. Last night's party was raucously discussed.

"People, please!" Solange said. "Is anyone even listening to me? *Any*one?"

I fumbled in my purse. "Here," I said, keeping my head turned sideways.

"*Thank* you," she said for the benefit of her friends. She dragged it through her tangled curls.

Kristin stepped closer. She shielded me with her body, hiding me from sight even though no one was paying attention.

"Really, it doesn't look that bad," she said in a whisper.

"That's because it's on me and not you," I said.

She bit her lip. This time she was honest enough not to deny it.

• • •

The chin hair had won the first round, and inwardly, I was shaken. A pimple I could deal with, or under-eye circles. Even a bad case of flatulence, because I could blame it on one of the football players. Hey, they were beefy guys.

But a chin hair was . . . grotesque. Aberrant. Manly, even, and one thing a Homecoming Queen was *not* supposed to be was manly. *Just look, honey, she's absolutely stunning. Skin like ivory, eyes like violets, and—what's that? A whisker? Oh, turn away! Turn away!*

I was especially worried about Blake, my boyfriend. Blake was going to escort me onto the field. He didn't play football, but he was a track star, so the football players were cool with him. Plus, he was dating me, which would give any guy status. I wasn't saying that to be conceited, either. Well, all right, maybe I was—but at least I was aware of it. That counted for something, didn't it?

Anyway, being a trophy girl wasn't all it was cracked up to be. Sometimes I wished I was just normal looking, or even ugly (although ugly in a not-absolutely-hideous sort of way), so that if anybody liked me, I'd know they were liking me for *me*. Blake said I was crazy, that he loved me inside and out. Still, I worried.

If I were in a wheelchair, I wouldn't have this problem.

If I had only one leg, or a wine-colored birthmark mottling half my face, my life would be so much easier. Or if not easier, then truer. Realer. I would be noble and good and devote myself to charities, like feeding the homeless at Saint Joe's. And I would say things like "But honestly, they give back to *me*. The vagrants couldn't care less if I was there. They have tons of volunteers. But the work I do? Ladling out the cabbage soup?" I'd place my hand on my heart. "It enriches my soul."

But I didn't have a wine stain, and both my legs were in full working order. And even if excessive facial hair did qualify me for sainthood, I actually didn't *want* to feed the homeless. Not that I wanted them to be hungry—that would be terrible—but maybe I could be the one to fix the cabbage soup instead of serve it. Yes, that's what I'd do. I would call Saint Joe's this weekend. Only maybe I'd suggest turkey and cheese on focaccia. Or baby quiches.

But tonight all I wanted was a crisp fall night and no pregame rain, because high heels and muddy sod were a guaranteed disaster. A bouquet of roses would be nice. And, natch, a hairless chin.

Instead I got a full-on smackdown from Scout Hopkins, Queen of Pure. I ran into her in the stairwell, me on my way out and Scout on her way in. We collided, and I went sprawling. A tampon flew from the partially zipped lower pocket at the bottom of my backpack.

"Yikesies," Scout said. "We don't want *that* scooting around." She scrambled for it and palmed it to me. The wrapper crinkled as I shoved it back in my pack.

"Sorry," I said. My face burned. "I'm such a spaz. Are you OK?"

"Oh, totally. Don't worry about it." She held out her hand and heaved me up. "So . . . are you ready for the big night?" Her smile was easy as she took me in, but it froze when she noticed my chin. Her eyes widened. Then she gamely pretended that nothing was wrong.

"Is your dress drop-dead gorgeous?" she said in a

74

rush. "I'm sure it is. I wanted to buy a new dress, but I was like, 'Can I really justify spending a hundred dollars when children in Africa are dying from AIDS?' So I bought mine at A.R.C."

Of course you did, I thought. A.R.C. stood for the Association of Retarded Citizens, and it was like the Salvation Army only without the bell. All the clothes came from donations.

"It's awesome, though," Scout went on. Her eyes strayed to my chin. "It's, um . . ." She jerked her eyes back. "It's turquoise and flowy, and I can wear my cowboy boots with it."

Cowboy boots? To Homecoming? Then again, maybe with the right accessories she could pull it off—sort of a flouncy, Western, bohemian look. Just as long as she didn't wear the tube socks.

"I've got some turquoise earrings from Santa Fe," I said. "You can borrow them if you want."

"Yeah? Thanks, Zelly." She shifted her weight. "What's your dress like?"

"It's Marc Jacobs," I said. "It's black."

"Oh wow," Scout said. "You're going to look

absolutely"—down dipped her eyes, and her voice grew uncertain—"beautiful."

"For God's sake, just *say* it," I snapped. "I've got a chin hair! Do you think I don't know?!"

"It's nothing to be ashamed of," Scout said quickly. "It's hardly noticeable."

"Uh-huh."

Her brain searched for something to say. "I had a cold sore once. It was terrible! It was on picture day last year—can you imagine?"

Yes, actually, because Kristin and I had chortled over it when we pored over our yearbooks.

Scout shrugged. "But I told myself, 'Oh well. Eventually you'll look back at this and laugh.'"

Like we did, I almost said. Although afterward, I'd felt bad, because my dad got cold sores, and I knew they really hurt.

"So don't worry," she said. "Just think of it as one of those nutty things." Her gaze drifted once more to my chin.

"Well, thanks for that," I said. "And now, not to be rude, but—"

Scout gasped.

"What?" I said.

"Nothing!"

My hand flew to my chin. "What? What is it?"

Gone was Scout's look of Christian charity, replaced by cow-eyed horror. "It . . . grew, while I was watching. It grew!"

My fingers found the hair. It had been a quarter-inch sliver; now it was as long as my thumb. And it had thickened. Surely I was wrong, but it seemed to twitch at my touch.

Scout backed away, clutching the gold cross she wore around her neck.

I stammered something about the nurse, and too much caffeine, and please-don't-please-don't tell. And then I fled.

Nurse Wells took one look at my chin hair and blanched the color of biscuit gravy. "You need to see a dermatologist," she said, scribbling me a sick pass. "Or an electrolysist. Or both." She ripped the pass from the pad and placed it on the table between us.

"Go home, Zelly. Heaven forbid you're contagious."
She gave a start. "Oh my God—is it *waving*?"

By the time I got home, the chin hair extended a
good three inches and was as thick as a mouse tail. If
I looked down, I could see it undulating. Sniffing the
air, searching its surroundings. Cold sweat slicked my
body. I longed to escape, but how could I when it was
part of my very self? I thought of the tapeworm story,
the urban legend of the boy strapped to a chair and
tempted with a roasted turkey. Out of his mouth
slithered a tapeworm, blind and pulpy.

"Zelly, is that you?" my stepmom called when I
came in through the back door. "Thank you *so* much
for unloading the dishwasher this morning—I didn't
get the chance to tell you." Her heels clicked in the
hall. "But why are you home so early? Why aren't you
at school?"

She came into the kitchen and saw the hair. She
shrieked and dropped her load of laundry.

I burst into tears. "Get it off me!" I wailed. "Get it
off!"

She snapped into efficiency mode. "Wax," she said firmly. "Come with me."

But the wax was no match. I could feel the hair tighten against the force of it, and when the wax pulled free, the hair remained. If anything, it was longer now. And more lustrous.

Next my stepmom tried plucking, but she had no more success than Kristin.

"Ow!" I bellowed as she abandoned the tweezers and tugged with bare hands.

She let go. Her chest heaved as she tried to catch her breath. "Now this is just plain silly," she said.

"I have Homecoming tonight," I moaned. "Why is this happening?"

Her mouth took on a determined twist, and she extracted a pair of nail scissors from the drawer by the sink. She put them back. She pulled out a giant pair of sewing scissors, gleaming and sharp.

I stepped back. "Um . . . what are you doing?"

"Don't think about it. Just close your eyes."

"Oh God," I said.

The chin hair lashed wildly. My stepmom caught

its tail. I felt a jerking at my chin as it struggled to get away.

"Do it quick, or I'm going to throw up!"

There was a snip, followed by a blissful stillness. Then a sliding, slicing, *growing* sound, a new heaviness tugging my skin.

"Oh crap," my stepmom said.

"It's back, isn't it?" I said.

My stepmom wobbled beside me. "Zelly, sweetie, I need a Scotch."

Alone in my room, I dialed Kristin's cell.

"Hold on," she said when she answered. "Let me go somewhere where I can talk." The noise of chatter receded. "'K, I'm back. Where *are* you?"

"Am I a horrible person?" I demanded. "Is this my punishment for being, you know, *me*?"

"What are you talking about?"

"I'm shallow—I admit it! I'm vain and I'm petty and I care about my appearance! I use Crest Whitestrips! I'm addicted to microdermabrasion!"

"Is this about your chin hair?" she asked.

"*It's down to my belly button,*" I hissed. "It just keeps . . . growing!"

"Whoa," Kristin said. "Are you shitting me?"

"It's like something out of *The Exorcist*!" My voice trembled. I was only barely holding on.

"OK, Zelly, this is a problem," Kristin said.

I didn't bother to reply.

"And you think . . . you think it's payback because you're beautiful?"

"No, I think it's payback because I *like* being beautiful. Because . . . maybe I'm not so nice to people who aren't."

"Oh, bull pootie. Who are you mean to just because they're ugly? I've never seen you be mean to ugly people."

"Maybe not to their faces. But behind their backs I sometimes say things."

"Well, so do I. So does everybody."

I gripped the phone.

She sighed. "Zel, get real. Name one person—*one* person—who doesn't laugh at people behind their backs."

"Jesus," I said promptly.

"*Zelly,*" Kristin said.

"OK . . . then Scout Hopkins." She was as close to Jesus as they came.

"Scout doesn't count," Kristin said.

"Yeah-huh," I said. "And by the way, I told her I'd lend her my turquoise earrings. If I give them to my stepmom to give to you, will you pass them on when you see her tonight?"

"When *I* see her? Why not when *you* see her?"

I gulped. The chin hair looped itself around my forearm, like a puppy dog wanting to be petted, and I swiped at it ferociously.

"Zelly, you're a good person," Kristin said. "In fact . . . sometimes it pisses me off that you're so beautiful and nice, too."

I wanted desperately to believe her. "When am I nice?"

"When you help Erica with trig, even though she smacks her gum. That time you made everybody let Lucy sit with us at lunch. Yesterday, when you stood in the hall talking to Barton Weaversley about *Star*

Trek, even though you've never watched an episode in your life."

"I didn't want to hurt his feelings."

"See?"

Hmm. *Star Trek* really was extremely geeky, but Kristin was right. I'd mentioned neither the bad costumes nor the ridiculous makeup.

"You can have opinions about things and still be basically decent, Zelly. I mean, come on. Why else would Blake love you so much?"

Blake, I thought, his name sending me back into panic. Outside, a car pulled into our drive. I dashed to the window to see who it was. Blake!

"Holy crap," I said to Kristin. "I've got to go!"

"Huh?" she said. "Why?"

"Thanks for the pep talk. Bye!" I tossed my phone on the bed and paced back and forth. How was I going to get rid of him? The chin hair reached the floor now, and it was as thick as twine. I almost tripped.

I heard the front door open, and I peered out of my window to see my stepmom cross over to Blake and give him a hug. Crouching down, I cracked the window so I could hear.

"—*love* your sweater," she was saying, stepping back to admire him from arm's length. "Is that what you're wearing to the game?"

"Is Zelly here?" Blake asked. "Someone said she'd gone home sick. Is she all right?"

"Oh dear," my stepmom said. "She's . . . well . . . I think she's a little concerned about her appearance. You know us ladies!"

"Can I go see her?" Blake said.

My stepmom hesitated. "I'm not sure she's—"

"Just for a sec," Blake said. He headed for the door.

"No!" I yelled.

He jumped, and so did my stepmom. They craned their necks upward.

Keeping the lower half of my face hidden, I said, "Don't you dare step through that door. If you step through that door, I will never speak to you again. I mean it!"

"Zelly, what's your problem?" Blake said.

My stepmom clasped her hands. "Okeydoke, I'll

just leave you kids to it," she said. She retreated into the house.

"Zel?" Blake repeated.

The chin hair nudged at the windowsill, trying to poke free.

"I'm having . . . a bad hair day," I said through gritted teeth.

"What are you talking about?" Blake said. "Your hair looks great."

He meant my shiny, honey-blond mane, which I kept radiant with flaxseed oil. But the chin hair took the compliment for itself, and in a spasm of joy it flipped up and over the wooden sill, unfurling to the ground below.

Blake gaped. "What the . . . ?"

Mortified, I tried to reel the hair back in.

"Just go!" I said to Blake. "There's something wrong with me. Please, just go!"

Blake straightened his spine. He strode toward my second-story window and grasped the chin hair, now thick as a rope. "Stay there," he said. "I'm coming up."

My eyes popped as he began climbing. "Ow ow

owww," I said, bracing myself against the wall with my knees.

Two sharp tugs, and the top of his head appeared. Another tug, and he heaved himself in, grunting as he tumbled over the sill. He righted himself and stared at the wreck of me.

"That's a really long chin hair," he said at last.

Shame washed over me. It came in a trembling wave and left me hollow.

"I'll understand if you don't want to go to Homecoming with me," I said. "Anyway, I'm not going. Scout Hopkins can have my crown!"

"But you're the queen," he said.

"As if!" I gestured at the chin hair, which had slithered back up the side of the house and lay pooled in my lap. I brushed it off me, but it coiled right back.

Blake tried unsuccessfully to hide his smile. "I think it likes you," he said.

"Aren't you grossed out?" I asked.

"Well . . . maybe," he admitted. "But I'm grossed out when you burp, too. Woo-doggie, you could knock a truck driver under the table."

"Blake!"

"Remember the time you had all those onion rings, and you nearly blasted my eyebrows off?"

"*Blake!*"

He grew serious. "Zelly, for real. What's a little chin hair between friends?"

"*Big* chin hair," I said.

"Fine. What's a frickin' enormous chin hair between friends?" He grabbed my hand and squeezed it. "And babe—we're going to Homecoming."

I snorted. "Oh no we're not."

"Oh yes we are. You wouldn't let the way you look stop you from having fun, would you?" He touched my nose. "That's not the Zelly I know."

"Please. It is so."

He laughed. "Well . . . it doesn't have to be, does it?"

I considered. Going to Homecoming with a full-length chin hair . . . it would kind of be like living in a yurt. Wouldn't it? Only with dancing afterward? And a crown? And no barley water?

"I *could* tie a ribbon on it, maybe," I said slowly. "To match my dress . . ."

Blake pulled me toward him. "That's my girl."

Tears welled in my eyes, because he *did* love me. He really did.

"You're so beautiful," I told him.

"*You're* the one who's beautiful," he replied.

I nestled against his chest, and he stroked my back. The chin hair wrapped around us, pulling us close.

SIDE-SHOW

Louise Hawes

His brother used to trap Payton the same way every time. "What a beauty!" Eddie would stretch out that last word, pulling it like a lure through still water. "You gotta see this!" And Payton would always believe, always follow after, eager to share his brother's latest miracle.

Lots of times, it was dead things. Eddie would stop a few feet ahead of Payton on the sidewalk. "Wow!" he'd say, standing above a dark shape in the gutter, then getting down on his haunches and staring fixedly. "C'mere, Pay."

Payton, four years younger and forever trying to narrow the margin, would run to catch up with his brother. Eddie's husky voice promised wonders: "Look at this, will ya?" Payton would stoop, a compliant shadow, and study the shape in the street. Often it was a squirrel, or a pigeon; once it had been a raccoon. A car had literally squeezed the life out of it. Payton had wanted to throw up, but he'd felt Eddie behind him, known without turning how his brother stood with his hands on his hips, his mouth tight and scornful. So he'd forced himself to look, to watch the upturned snout, the flies congregating around the jelly of the open eyes.

He had run home that day, and raced upstairs to his mother's room. In the dark, he'd opened one of her dresser drawers. Sobbing, he'd patted the filmy clouds of stockings, inhaled the gardenia scent of her sachet, and lifted a cool silk slip to his face.

The sideshow would be different, though. Payton was sure of it. He was older now, after all, and the whole thing had been his idea. A traveling circus had set up on the Little League field, and the posters were all over town: BRAND NEW FOR 1954! HANDEE'S MUTANTS AND MONSTERS! The sideshow boasted such "Mystifying Mistakes of Nature" as a Fat Woman (her picture showed her balanced in a scale opposite a blue pickup), a five-legged calf, and a Wildman who ate metal and had to be kept behind bars like an animal.

But it wasn't any of these misfits that interested Payton, who often felt like a mistake himself, glabrous and unfinished beside his lean, confident brother. It was the Tattooed Lady he'd set his heart on seeing. Her poster was the largest of all: It showed her standing, hands on hips, smiling with pride at her magnificently decorated skin.

There were kittens on her arms, a jungle scene on her belly; there were lilies and Chinese dragons and exploding volcanoes—all in commanding, vibrant hues. Most astonishing, loveliest of all, Payton thought, was the green-and-yellow cobra, its hood spread wide, its ruby eyes flashing, that crawled from the lucky lady's left foot to the top of her thigh.

But Payton didn't tell Eddie about the kittens or the jungle; he knew how the game was played. "They're freaks," he said, knowing the seduction the word held for his brother. "Freaks of nature."

Eddie pretended not to be interested, but Payton saw the way he forgot himself for a second, the way his eyes widened. So Payton persisted, begged for three days straight, until, finally, the deal was struck. He swore he would be his brother's slave for a month, no backsies, if Eddie would help him sneak into the show.

Even though he was almost twelve and had begun to think of himself as a teenager, Payton was too young to view legally what waited behind the striped tent flap at the back of the fairgrounds. So, persuaded by the fact that slaves not only had to do your bidding but would also keep quiet about what time you snuck back home from seeing Ella Louise Baines, Eddie paid and went into the tent without his kid brother.

From there, he had promised to scuttle along the canvas, looking for cover. His search probably took only a few moments, but the wait seemed endless to Payton, who remained faithfully rooted to the spot he'd been assigned outside. Finally, Eddie ducked behind a providential trash barrel, lifted the tent's hem, and whistled with one finger the way Payton never could.

Once inside, Payton found he was shorter than everyone else and had to walk on his toes, straining to see over shoulders, around heads. There were more people in the tent than he'd expected, mostly men, all laughing loudly and pointing. Disappointed in the five-legged calf, whose fifth leg was little more than a stringy extra tail, he and Eddie joined the crowd around the Fat Woman's metal folding chair. The men jostled and nudged one another with their elbows. "Boy, that's a mountain of love," shouted one. "I'd sure as hell want topsies with her!"

The woman sat for their inspection, insulated by her shiny folds. Lost in the flesh of her face, two small eyes stared out impassively at her tormentors. "Where'd you get that dress?" someone beside Payton yelled. "The circus lend you a tent?" Payton turned to see Eddie, felled by his own cleverness, doubled over with laughter.

Payton, who was used to Eddie's teasing, suspected that the Fat Woman, too, knew how to take words that were hurled at her and turn them into a sort of music, a loud, bristling symphony that, if you focused, got fainter and fainter until it hardly mattered at all. So he and the woman waited until Eddie had had enough, until he led his brother away from the crowd and they moved at last toward the pale green curtain where Payton's favorite poster was hung.

When they saw her, though, the Tattooed Lady was the biggest disappointment of all. She was such a letdown, in fact, that Payton tugged on his brother's shirt until Eddie turned around. When he had the older boy's attention, Payton complained, indignantly and much too loudly, as if he'd suddenly mastered Eddie's cynicism, "She's not like the picture at all!"

And she wasn't. None of the intricate wonders on the poster had been reproduced on this woman's sallow, lifeless flesh. She sat, rather than stood, as if even she knew she had nothing to show off. She wore a stiff, corseted bathing suit like the one Payton and Eddie's mother put on once a year when the family went to Kreller's Amusement Park and Swim Land. Covering the parts of the woman that weren't hidden by the suit was a jumble of blotches that had, undoubtedly, once been separate tattoos. But they had long ago lost most of their colors and run together in a sort of purple rash.

Here and there, Payton could pick out the faded suggestion of a howling wolf or letters that still yearned, vaguely, to spell something—a name, maybe? But there were no volcanoes, no rain forests, and, though he checked every surface except the undersides of the woman's legs, no bright and rippling cobra like the one that had figured so prominently in the poster.

When the Tattooed Lady finally looked up at them, then turned away to spit, like a man, on the ground beside her camp stool, Eddie pushed Payton back toward the curtain. "C'mon, Pay," he said.

"There's stuff way better than this."

Payton let his brother lead him away, followed him to a new crowd that had formed around another exhibit. Surprisingly, though, these men were all silent. Not one laughed or pointed or dug his elbow into his neighbor's ribs. The girl they watched was painting with her teeth.

Even if the men had yelled or stamped, Payton decided, the girl couldn't have heard them. She and her canvas and paints were sealed away from them in a small glass booth, where, he hoped, the smells of cotton candy and elderly apples glazed with syrup couldn't reach her.

She was young, not much older than Eddie. Payton, who stared in wonder at her lovely, flushed face, at first thought the girl was behind glass because she was so beautiful. He had a box at home, a velvet-covered heart that had once held chocolates. He'd rescued it from the trash and used it to save things he liked to look at, things he wanted to keep forever. The girl in the booth wasn't splashy and loud like the poster of the Tattooed Lady, or sparkly and hard like

Eddie's girl, with her perfectly arched and penciled brows. This girl was softer than that—a tune hummed instead of sung; a dream you couldn't remember when you woke up; a pale, small-faced violet poking through moss. Payton stood for a full minute, spellbound in front of the glass, before he realized the girl he was staring at had no arms or legs.

Her torso was strapped to a cushioned chair, and she was dressed in a pink cotton blouse, its empty sleeves hanging limp at her sides. The bottom of the blouse, under the black strap at her waist, was folded and neatly draped over the cushion.

Payton willed her to look up, but she ignored the faces trained on her. It was as if he and the rest of the crowd didn't exist, as if they stood behind a one-way mirror, their stares and whispers bouncing off the glass. The girl concentrated on her work instead, never once taking her eyes from the tangle of flowers and leaves on the canvas propped in front of her chair.

Gently, methodically, her lips closed around the tapered handle of a paintbrush. As if she were sipping from a straw, she sucked it from a forest of palette knives and brushes in a drinking glass on the table beside her. Next, she dipped the brush into a pot of paint, like one of the stolid, round jars Payton had used in kindergarten.

Her eyes nearly closed as she stroked glistening red along the canvas. Everywhere her brush touched, a bright rose blossomed like sudden blood. Her lips trembled and puckered, and the quick flowers bloomed in miraculous patches. Payton watched, mesmerized, until Eddie broke the spell. "God," he said, sounding strangely awed, "that gimp sure can paint, can't she?"

It was then Payton started to imagine what the girl looked like under her pink blouse. Warm and guilty, he pictured breasts and pubic hair floating under the sheer fabric. A body that couldn't do anything, a body you could do anything to.

He tried to shake off the nauseating sweetness, the sticky residue coating his throat and nostrils. He wondered if the girl had heard Eddie, if she felt where the men's eyes burnt holes in her cropped body. He wondered what he could ever do to deserve arms, to be worthy of legs. Until the heat in the small tent filled his chest. Until the light glancing off the girl's glass cage made him dizzy. Until he ran outside, crouched behind the tent, and threw up blue cotton candy all over the ground.

Afterward, Eddie, who didn't need to consult his slave on their agenda, and wouldn't, in all likelihood, have checked with Payton anyway, dragged him off so they could get their pictures taken. They found one of those souvenir photographers, where you stick your head through a cardboard hole so your face appears on top of a cartoon body. "Come on," Eddie yelled over the music from the flying tea cups. "I want to be a pirate."

It was like walking into the dreary, echoing cistern near school, to come into the photographer's tent from the noise and light outside. The last thing Payton wanted to do was to stand in this half-light while his brother pawed through the painted boards.

"Here's a good one for you, Pay," Eddie called from the back of the musty tent. He held up a board with a monkey's body on it. The monkey was swinging from a tree and holding a banana up to its mouth. "Yeah, that's you, all right," Eddie said, chuckling. His voice was loud, self-conscious. "C'mere."

Dizzy with the thick, sad smells, nursing shame, Payton did as he was told. Dutifully, he bent his head through the hole in the cardboard, then sat down on a small stool behind it. The photographer, an old man with veined hands and pants that spilled over the tops of his shoes, held up a mirror to show him what he looked like.

Payton sat on the stool and stared at his monkey body in the glass. At his own burning face, and behind that at Eddie's smile, distant and amused. "Payton, the monkey," Eddie said from the summit of his sixteen years. "Payton, the Ape Boy!" At first, encouraged by his brother's anguish, he upped the ante. "Come one, come all," he hollered. "He's got a face like your backside and a backside that lights up at Christmas." Glancing for a minute at the photographer for approval, he hurried on. "Yessir, yessir! Payton, the Freak of Nature. Don't get too close, folks. He might just bite off your arm." That was when Payton started to cry.

And once he started, he couldn't stop. It was as if his grief were a thing apart; as if the harsh, dog-like yelps were coming from someone else. Even though Eddie specialized in the fine art of bringing his younger brother to tears, the sudden, eruptive force of Payton's misery seemed to bother him. "Aw, Pay," he kept saying, shifting from one sneak-ered foot to the other. "Come on, Pay. I didn't mean nothing."

Still sobbing, but on the wind-down, Payton watched a strangely penitent Eddie shuffle over to the photographer. "This is kid stuff," Eddie told the photographer, helping Payton to duck his head, lifting off the yoke of the board. "Me and my brother, we'll just take a picture like we are." Then, as if his kindness embarrassed him, he added, "It's for our mother. She'd like it better plain."

So they'd posed together, and Payton, tears drying on his face, had felt the weight of his brother's arm around him. As if they were two friends, two careless boys together out of choice, not bound by the strange and oppressive ties of brotherhood.

When they took the photograph home, their mother wanted to glue it in the scrapbook, but Payton begged to keep it instead. That night before he fell asleep, he pulled the candy box from under his bed. He held the new picture for a while, staring at it in the moonlight coming through the blinds, memorizing the sweet curve of his brother's arm around his own small shoulders. Finally, he removed the velvet top of the box and put the photo inside with his other treasures—the mysterious, crenulated nest of a paper wasp; the featureless, pancaked quarter some boys had left on a railroad track; the pale, frosted wing of a luna moth; and a whole family of Guatemalan worry people with bendable wire bodies and tiny, smiling faces, each no bigger than the head of a match.

WHAT I Look LIKE

Jamie Pittel

The Saturday after Thanksgiving, Carrie pierces my nose. Afterward, I sit on the floor of her bedroom in a kind of daze. There's something— blood?—trickling from the inside of my nose. The needle is still sticking into me, and the numbness from the ice we held against my nose earlier is starting to fade. It hurts. This dull, deep pain that centers on the needle and spreads to my whole head. My eye is watering uncontrollably, and I have to hold my hand against it so the tears don't fall onto my nose.

"Here, Blondie." Carrie is at my side, offering me a fresh ice cube wrapped in a paper towel.

There isn't an easy place to hold the ice. Any contact will make my nose hurt worse. I settle on holding it against the bottom of my nostril, making it impossible to breathe through my nose. It doesn't hurt less, but the cold feels good, makes me a little more alert.

"Are you OK?" she says.

I nod. "I think so." Then I laugh.

"You're laughing," Carrie says. "Which means either you're OK or you're delirious. Either way, now would be a good time to put in the hoop."

We bought a real body-piercing hoop, the kind that's supposed to be safe and sterile and all that. I have no idea how I'm going to get the needle out of my nose and the hoop in without fainting, but I nod anyway. Now would probably be better than later.

I squeeze my eyes shut and clutch onto the bottom of my sweater with both hands, dropping my ice cube on the carpet. When she pulls the needle away, it hurts less for a second, then I feel her poking around with the hoop for the hole, twisting it into my skin, and this wave of something so unlike what I understand pain to be shoots through my head. Blood rushes under my skin faster than usual, like it's trying to push my limbs to move. I'm not going to faint. Instead it's like I have *more* strength. Like if Carrie were really trying to hurt me rather than improve my image, I could kill her with my bare hands.

"There," she says, after twisting the hoop impossibly to get it hooked closed. "Try not to touch it except when you wash it—just with soap. Then turn it a little so it doesn't heal stuck."

I nod. Deep breath. I stand, pulling myself up by the leg of the desk chair, hand-over-hand like I'm climbing a mountain. I'm shocked when I get to the mirror on the back of Carrie's door.

I look exactly the same.

In two and a half weeks I'll be going to see my mother for winter break. It's been almost six months since I moved to New York to live with my dad. I feel so different, it seems like she shouldn't even recognize me when I go back to Berkeley, but the reality is, she might not even notice this when I first get off the plane. I mean, I just look like me. Me, straight blond hair that I cut short right after Halloween. Me in faded, slightly-too-small jeans and my father's blue V-neck sweater. You notice these things—the clothes—before my nose. It's still there, pretty small, round at the end, and on one side there's a delicate silver hoop. The most normal thing in the world. It's not even red or swollen like it should be. "Huh." I cross my arms, turn my head to the side to see the hoop better.

"Do you like it?" Carrie asks.

I nod. "Yeah, I do. It's just not all that dramatic, you know?"

My nose is throbbing, and my whole head is slightly sore. What I'm feeling is bored. Like I thought this would entertain me and now it doesn't.

"If you want dramatic," Carrie says, "we could do something else."

I sigh. "I don't think I could handle any more pain right now."

106

She shakes her head. "Come here." She motions for me to follow her and pushes open the door to her brother Ben's room without knocking. My ears are hit by a blast of electric guitar and drums and some sort of screechy vocals. Carrie takes an orange sneaker to the head.

Ben's sitting on his mattress in the corner of the room. "Knock, dumb-ass," he yells over the music, waving his second sneaker menacingly in one hand. "I did not invite you into my lair."

"Over here," Carrie says to me, ignoring Ben. She points to a bookcase that's cluttered with partly full jars of different colors. Hair dye. There's a sludgy green, traffic-light yellow, peacock blue, inky black, the ruby red I saw on both Ben and Carrie when I first met them. Today Ben's hair is teal. Carrie's is her natural caramel color. It's grown out long enough to show that she has curls, which are pushed out of the way with five or six barrettes, randomly placed on either side of her head.

"My hair?" I say, still feeling kind of woozy. She's right. Even short, my hair is boring. I mean, Gus has a four-inch-tall Mohawk—he's probably embarrassed to be seen with me.

"He-ee-ey," Ben says, standing up now and moving in front of his bookcase to turn the music down. "Blondie." He looks at me like he just noticed I'm standing here. "You pierced your nose."

I nod. He isn't asking, just noticing out loud. It took him about three minutes. Too long.

"It looks cool," he says.

Carrie works her way behind him to dig through the jars of dye. "Swamp Green?" she calls to me.

"Not." I cross my arms against my chest and lean into the door frame.

"Wouldn't have thought you could pull it off," Ben says, looking at me sideways. "You're starting to look like a halfway-normal person."

"Normal, thank you. That's just what I was going for." I push Ben aside and look over Carrie's shoulder at the dyes. "What else is there?"

"Blueberry?" She holds the almost-full jar up against my hair.

"Oh yes," I say. "I think Blueberry is just the thing. Blueberry is absolutely the epitome of normal."

Carrie grins. "You sure?"

"Yep." My nose is hurting less already at the prospect of blue hair. "I really, really want Blueberry."

"Your parents are so going to freak."

I shrug. "Not my dad."

"You're seeing your mom at Christmas?"

I nod. "No avoiding it."

"Let's go, then."

I turn the blue jar around in my hand, hold it in the light to see the color sparkle through the glass. "Yeah. Let's."

Watching the blue stream of water rush down the kitchen drain, getting more and more transparent, feeling the blood fill up my head and my nose ache like it's going to fall off, I'm pretty sure people will notice a difference. When the water's finally clear, I flip my hair back and drip onto my shoulders and the linoleum.

Carrie hands me a towel and I rub down my head, smiling because I feel clean and energized. I raise my eyebrows. "So is it really blue?"

Ben laughs. "Change your mind already?"

I shake my head and try to look at my reflection in the glass door of the microwave. Too dark to see. I go check the bathroom mirror.

This is noticeable. I peer into the mirror, turn my head to one side and then the other. The person I'm looking at is like me, but not me. She's like my long-lost twin sister who's much more worldly than I am. She probably plays pool and lives in a loft with her sheepdog and listens to blues music in smoky clubs and eats sushi. Her friends are poets and sculptors and bass players—the kind of people my mother has never even met.

Carrie reaches for a pot of hair goo on the sink next to me and scoops some into her palm. "You can't have hair that color falling into your face, you know." She sweeps her hands through my hair, smoothing it back so it's slick and sticky. My head looks like a blue bowling ball.

"We should go out," Ben says. We're all squeezed into the bathroom now, crowded around the sink.

"And celebrate," says Carrie.

"Absolutely," says me.

I call Gus, and we meet at Riverside Park and crowd onto one of those kiddie merry-go-rounds that you spin around until everyone's dizzy and nauseated. Right now it's not moving except to creak and tilt whenever someone shifts positions.

"I propose a toast." Gus holds up the bottle of Southern Comfort we've been sharing. "To Lisa's blueness." He takes a sip from the bottle and hands it to me. "May she shock the pants off her mother."

Everyone laughs. I choke on the sweet liquor and pass the bottle to Ben, trying not to cough because it stretches my face and makes my nose hurt.

"She's going to die," I say. "She used to dress me in *outfits*."

Gus laughs. "Outfits! Good thing you got away."

He's kidding, but I really was running away from the outfits. Last summer, my mom and I were both brides-maids in my aunt's wedding—matching lavender

dresses, baby's breath in our hair, the whole deal—
and I was this miniature version of her, which I realized I had always, *always* been. I had no idea what I
would look like if I dressed myself. I moved away
because I needed to find out.

Carrie hands me a carton of ice cream with a plastic
spoon sticking out of it. "What did your parents do?"
I wave the spoon at the three of them. "About, you
know, the punk stuff?"

"Mom expects it," Carrie says.

Ben nods. "Nothing she can do."

I take a bite of ice cream and it swims down into
my alcohol-warmed belly and chills me.

"Mine think it's a fucking miracle," Gus says.
"They think I'm like one of the artists at their snooty-
ass gallery. They don't know shit."

Will my mother yell? Will she disown me? Hold
me down and pour peroxide over my head? I can't
imagine her anything but confused. She would never
expect this of me. Before the bridesmaid incident, I
just wore her outfits, all cheerful-like. When I was
little, I kind of loved it—going shopping together,

getting the same haircuts and showing them off to my dad when we got home. Now she won't know who I am. Which of course she already doesn't. When she sees me, she'll *know* she doesn't know.

I lean closer into Gus's side and reach my arm out to take the bottle back from Carrie, who's drinking now, tilting it back into her mouth, her head resting on one of the bars of the merry-go-round.

"Blondie," she says when she sits up and sees me beckoning for a drink, "you're turning into a little bottle hog."

"I'm cold," I say. "And I'm not blond."

Gus laughs and points at Carrie. "She's got you there."

Carrie rolls her eyes and slaps Gus's hand out of her face. "You will always be blond," she says, looking me right in the eye. "You can't change something like that."

I pretend to ignore her, but those words stay with me all night. They flit around in my head, my liquid brain, working slower and stranger with the alcohol. *Always blond.* I twist my good-luck braid—the only f my hair—around my pinky until it

ulation, the tip of my finger purple

...... I pull a strand of blue down into my face, roll it between my thumb and index finger until the brittleness from the gel flakes away and it's dry and soft and peacock colored. The blue doesn't rub off on my fingers. *You can't change something like that.*

I wake up at five thirty. Everything hurts. My nose most of all, but also my head, my stomach. The Southern Comfort is still with me.

My father smelled it on me when I came home, looked back and forth from my nose to my hair. Waved a hand in front of his nose. "You smell like a distillery, Lisa." He sniffed. "And cigarettes?"

"I don't smoke," I said. "Just my friends were smoking around me."

"I'm supposed to celebrate *that?*" he said, gesturing to the rest of me. When I didn't have an answer, he sighed. "We'll talk about it in the morning, Lise. But you're going to have to tell your mother. About all of it."

He's still asleep. My mother will be asleep for

hours and hours in California. I drink three cups of water in a row, the glass cool against my lower lip, clicking loud on my teeth. I bring a fourth cup into the bathroom with me and stand in front of the mirror again. Pale, pale skin—impossible to remember June in Berkeley when I was so brown and so blond—hair now the color of blueberry Kool-Aid, sticking up in tufts in the back of my head. Silver metal runs right through the flesh of my nostril, just punched in there like the rings on my binder. The mirror draws me to it, like a hand pulling me back every time I turn away. I close my eyes and sip my water, open them and look again. I still look like this. This is what I look like. All the time.

As soon as it's late enough in California, I call my mother.

"Hello, darling," she says. "I miss you."

"Yeah," I say. I stop for a minute, breathe, listen to her breathing three thousand miles away. "I miss you, too." I do, and I listen for a minute while she talks all businesslike and chatty about her Thanksgiving leftovers, realizing this is the last time she'll ever be this nice to me. This is the last moment she'll think I belong to her. She can't see me yet.

"Mom, I have to tell you something."

"Oh. What is it, darling?"

"Well, a few things, actually. Remember how I got my hair cut short a while ago? I told you that, right?"

"Yes."

"Well, I was still wanting, you know, a change. To look different from before."

"Yes?" Her voice is getting impatient.

"So I colored it." She's rubbing off on me. I would *never* have used the word "colored" about my hair if I was talking to anyone else.

"Oh?"

"Blue."

"*What?*" She's screeching.

"Blue. I *dyed* my hair blue. Also I pierced my nose."

"You pierced . . ." She's so confused she can't form whole sentences. "You *what?*"

"My nose. There's a hoop in it. Not in the middle, like cattle. I think that's disgusting. Mine's just on one side. It looks really good, Mom. I like how it looks."

"I see," she says. There's a scary calm to her voice.

Either she's still in shock, or she's already decided to disown me and isn't even upset.

I take a big breath. "So Dad wanted me to tell you, also, that last night, after I did all that, I went out, you know, with my friends."

"Yes?" Her yesses just pull me along, like she's actually tugging at the phone cord, bringing me closer and closer to her so she can make some sense of what I'm telling her.

"And we were out pretty late, I guess. And I was drinking. I came home kind of drunk, and Dad was really mad at me. He wanted me to tell you."

There's this chilly silence, until finally she says, "Lisa, let me talk to your father." Her enunciation is astounding.

"He's out. He went to get groceries. Do you want me to have him call you when he gets back?"

"No," she says, all clippy. "No, that's all right. Just tell him . . . tell him I'll talk to him tomorrow."

"OK, Mom." I wait to see if she's going to say anything else, but she's just breathing again, so far away. "Mom, how mad at me are you? Because I thought you'd be really mad, but you're not saying anything.

Are you so mad you're not speaking to me?"

"No, sweetie," she says, her voice all fake-nice again. "I'm not mad. Concerned. We'll talk about this more tomorrow, OK?" It's like she's telling this to herself as much as me. She'll call back tomorrow when she's decided how to deal with me. After she's yelled at my dad, she'll yell at me. I can wait.

"She probably had to consult her hairdresser about how to put you back the way you were," Carrie says at school on Monday. "And tonight she'll call you back and explain how you can pretend this ugliness never happened."

I glare at her. " 'Ugliness'? You think I look ugly?"

She shakes her head and pulls her French book out of her locker. "No, I think you look great. You know what I mean. Like, from her point of view, the whole *situation* is ugly."

"Yeah, I know what you mean." But maybe I *do* look ugly. I was so worried about looking different, I forgot about pretty. What does Gus think?

I meet him at Gray's Papaya after school. We lean

against the wall outside, drinking smoothies. My hands sweat inside mittens, even wrapped around the cold waxed-paper cup.

"Gus?" I tap the thick sole of one of his Doc Martens with the toe of mine.

"Hmm." He raises his head to look at me, lips still wrapped around his straw.

"So I look really different now. I mean, I must look like a totally different person from when we started going out?"

Gus raises his eyebrows and nods slightly. "Uh-huh. You look different."

"Is that weird?"

He puts his cup down on the sidewalk and stands in front of me, lifts my chin up with his hand and looks straight at me. His rings are cold against my skin. With the other hand he brushes my cheek along the right side of my nose, near my nose ring. "Does it still hurt?"

"Some. A little less." I wrinkle my eyebrows. "You're not answering me, Gus. Do you hate how I look now?"

He shakes his head, his face still inches from mine.

"No. I think it's good."

"You think it *is* good, like on some big philosophical level, or you think it *looks* good?"

He kisses me on the lips, his hands still cupping my face. "Both."

That's the right answer. So why am I disappointed? Maybe I want to challenge Gus, too. To see if he's still attracted to me if I don't look as good. Because maybe he liked me *because* I was blond and normal looking and, I guess, pretty in this kind of conventional way. Unlike the other people he hangs out with.

"You're frowning." He drops his hands.

I press my lips together. "Gus, why do you like me?"

He picks up his smoothie and takes a long sip. "You're not bored," he says. He drinks more and looks at me sideways without raising his head all the way.

"What?"

"I like you, among other reasons, because you're not bored."

I narrow my eyes and walk to the corner to throw out my empty cup.

He follows and throws his away, even though it's half full. "Everyone I know is bored, Lise. Except you. Look at Ben and Carrie. School bores them. Adults bore them. Hell, we bore them." He kicks the garbage can and steps back to our spot against the wall. "My parents think they can get unbored by discovering new talent. They find some supposedly fascinating new artist and show him off to the world and then, when they're still bored, they go look for another one.

"But *you* are totally unbored. You're, like, engaged with the world. All the time. You didn't do this"—he wraps a strand of my hair around his index finger— "because you were bored with being blond, right? You did it because you were *interested* in being blue."

I smile, because it would be great if that were true. But is it?

"Come on." He tugs at my jacket and steps away from the wall.

"Where?"

"The gallery."

I look at him like a question mark.

"Yeah. I'm thinking maybe you won't hate it."

• • •

From the street it looks like nothing—a glass door interrupting a white stucco wall. Inside it's all spare white space, white walls spotted with shapes of color.

A mechanical *ding-dong* sounds overhead as we walk through the door, and a tall man with thinning black hair and thick black glasses appears from behind one of the freestanding extrawhite walls.

"That couldn't possibly be my son? Is the apartment on fire? Do you need money?" He winks at me while Gus glares.

I press my lips together to keep from smiling and lean into Gus's side.

He sighs. "Dad, this is Lisa." He's mumbling, like a whole different person.

"Ah." His father steps forward and takes my right hand in both of his. "I've heard nothing at all about you. What a pleasure."

He and Gus stare each other down for a minute, and I wait, trying to figure out how real the tension is. Maybe sarcastic is just what they do.

"You must be an artist," his dad says.

"Um, not really."

"That's not why you're here, then? Hmph." He crosses his arms against his chest and looks at me.

Gus squeezes my hand but doesn't say a word.

"I think you *are* an artist." He gestures at my head. "That's your canvas right there."

I don't understand for a minute. But then I do. My hair, he means. My nose. That's what people see now when they see me.

He waves his hand for me to follow him to one of the display walls. "Take a look around, Lisa-who-I've-never-heard-of."

Gus gives his father a violent look.

"Maybe something will inspire you."

I step back, away from both of them. "I'll just look, then?"

They shrug identical bony shoulders.

I walk up one side of the room, turn a corner, walk along another wall. The air around me feels thin, white like the walls. I stare at each piece, but nothing happens. I feel Gus and his father watching me, waiting for a reaction. This is a test. I have to prove to

Gus that I'm interested in this stuff, not bored by it, but also I have to be on his side in the fight he's having with his dad. And for his father, I have to fall in love with the right piece so he can proclaim me an artist.

Gus leans against a bare patch of wall with his arms crossed, staring at me. His dad is pacing, leaving a few feet between us so he can pretend he's not following me around.

To escape both of them, I turn into this small room off the main gallery, and now I *want* to look at the art. Tables are scattered around the room—all different sizes and heights—and ledges stick out of the walls. On each surface is a wooden box, painted white or green or pale pink or gold. They have writing on them, black letters, done, I think, with stamps or stencils. One huge round box has stories on it, random paragraphs from fairy tales. "The Ugly Duckling" covers the inside—not all of it, but the part where the ugly duckling first sees the other swans and he wants to be with them, even though he doesn't know why. Other boxes have poems or dreams or just one word, repeated again and again, letters snaking around the edges of the wood.

Now *I* want to write words on boxes. On walls, T-shirts, furniture. My fingers itch to write words. I step from one box to the next, reading every word, touching the corners to feel the texture of the paint, opening lids to find more words inside. Then a hand is on my shoulder, and I startle and gasp out loud.

"Sorry," Gus says.

"I like these," I whisper.

He nods.

"Maybe you're a poet," says his father, who is standing in the doorway to this little room full of boxes. "A word sculptor."

"'A word sculptor,'" I echo. "So my hair isn't why I'm an artist?"

"Could be it's just fashion," says Gus.

"You don't think fashion is art?" argues his father.

"You know," I say, "I should really get home. I mean, I told my dad I'd be home for dinner, and he doesn't know I'm here, and I shouldn't be late today, you know, after Saturday."

"Yeah," says Gus. "Let's get out of here."

I wave as Gus leads me toward the front door. "It was nice to meet you."

And we're back out on the street. It's dark now, and cold enough to see my breath under the streetlights.

"Did you see that big box," I say as we walk. "The one with the fairy tales?"

"Uh-huh."

We walk into the subway station, and it's too crowded to talk. Everyone is coming home from work, and Gus and I can barely stay together going down the stairs and through the turnstile, much less talk, until we get to our platform.

"The box?" he says.

"Right," I continue, almost shouting. "It had part of 'The Ugly Duckling' on it. You know that story?"

"Yeah, sure. Beauty is in the eye of the beholder and all that."

"Right. But when I was looking at it, I was thinking that's not what it's really about. I mean, it's not about beauty."

"No?"

"Nope. Not at all. It's really about the difference

between who you really are and who you're *supposed* to be, like, according to your family."

"Yeah . . ."

"So this guy, he was born to a family of ducks, right? And he was supposed to be beautiful or cute or whatever, in a duckish way. Everyone expects him to be. But he's not, so they're disappointed in him."

"Until he finds out he's a swan."

"Right. But he still can't hang out with his family. He has to get away from the other ducks and be beautiful among swans. It's just like us, like everyone."

Our train comes and we step on, squeeze together against a pole, and I keep talking, loud, right into Gus's ear.

"My mom wants me to be pretty and well dressed in this really conservative, pale-pink way. She expects me to be, because she is. Like the ducks. She thinks I'm *wrong* because I'm not a duck. Your dad thinks how you look is cool, but he thinks it's because you're an artist. A duck. But you've got a swan Mohawk, not a duck Mohawk."

Gus grins at me, huge dimples in both cheeks. He's about to start laughing.

"I'm serious. Let me finish."

He nods, undoes his smile.

"All of us, you and me and all our friends, are swans. We're beautiful or special or whatever when we're together, but not in the way our families want us to be. They can't see it, because they think we're supposed to be like them. That's what the story's about."

We crawl off the train and up three flights of stairs to the street.

"So by your theory," Gus says, "our parents think we're ugly ducklings; our friends know we're beautiful swans."

"Exactly."

We turn onto my block and I walk more slowly, scraping my shoes along the sidewalk.

There's a woman standing on my front stoop, right under the halo of the porch light. I drag my feet slower, but she still gets closer. Her back is straight, a brown scarf matches her shoes, suitcase at her feet.

Swan. My mother is beautiful. A swan. Which makes me not. Either.

She sees me, furrows her carefully groomed eyebrows, tilts her head forward a bit farther to be sure it really is her daughter coming toward her.

I'm colder now inside my body than out. It's cold in my stomach; cold blood pumps from my heart. I squeeze Gus's hand tight, stop walking. Stand still.

"What?" Gus strokes the back of my hand with his thumb, doesn't try to loosen my grip.

Breathless, I open my mouth and close it again. I look at the sidewalk: grainy gray cement, not smooth.

"My mother," I whisper to the sidewalk, loosening my fingers but not letting go. "Over there."

Gus draws in his breath. "Oh."

I step forward. Lift my right foot, place it down, left foot up, down. Again. Eyes on my shoelaces, on the cracked, bumpy sidewalk. I stop when the stairs up to my front door are at my toes. Gus's left foot stops against my right. Our four Doc Martens make parallel lines, black, black, silver, silver. I raise my head.

She holds a hand against her cheek, leather glove against her pink skin, blond hair falling gracefully across the leather. Eyes blue like mine, peeking over her smooth brown fingers. They pierce into me, question, greet, scold, soothe.

"Darling."

"Mom."

Gus lets go of my hand.

Then my mom walks down the steps and reaches her arm out to hug me. I let her, and I feel Gus step away from me, giving her room. Briefly, I put my arms around her. A small squeeze to counter the big one she's giving me.

Then, gently, I push her away.

"Lisa, honey, look at you." Her voice soft, sad. "You don't look like you anymore."

"I do," I say. "I look just like me." All the fear drains out of me at the sound of my own voice. It's like the rush of strength I felt when Carrie put in my nose ring. I am sure now. Sure that this is the important part. Not shocking my mother or being beautiful—duck beautiful or swan beautiful. I reach behind me for Gus's hand. I can't see him, but I know he'll be there. And he is, fingers twisting around mine, no gloves in the way, just skin.

"This is what I look like, Mom."

J. James Keels

I got hair on my chest,
I look good without a shirt . . .

And I'm goin' out west
Where they'll appreciate me.

—Tom Waits, "Goin' out West"

I was nicknamed Ape the first day of ninth grade, in the locker room.

The showers were lined up in a row, shooting out

scalding water. I wore a white T-shirt, and hairs poked out like tiny black quills. I passed stall after stall, each shower with a boy, herded in like cattle, under its gallows nozzle. I walked for an eternity, until I reached the end of the row, turned the faucet, and stepped into the spray. Praying no one would notice. *Please God,* I pleaded, *don't let them see me.* I gazed at the empty lockers through the dense steam; everything seemed so far away.

Closing my eyes, I stood with my back to the others. I curled into myself, a sort of standing fetal position. My wet T-shirt clung to me; the white cotton revealed a dark pelt underneath. I felt the wet hair on my back, like a thin hump. I sensed their eyes on me, each set adding weight until I wanted to crumple to the ground from the pressure. I turned around and found only *one* set of eyes, staring right into mine.

Jason Keller, all-star quarterback, pointed and uttered his historic words—words that would follow me into my sophomore year.

Look at the Ape!

• • •

I am fully dressed, yet I stretch out on my back, on top of the already-made covers. Rolling onto my side, I look at the mirror on the bureau. My bushy hair hides sleep-deprived eyes. I look like a sideshow carny: *Ford, the Ape-Faced Boy—fifty cents for a gander!*

"It's time, Ford," I mutter into my pillow.

Ford Gordon. It sounds terrible—even I hate saying it. All the hard "o's" and everything. I was named after the car manufacturer. I wish my mom had been fooling, but my name is for real. Long story short, my grandfather strong-armed her in the delivery room.

"At least give *your* son a fighting chance. Don't give him a Greek name." So Ford it was—as American as apple pie. *Ford Gordon.* My name is based on a myth. American cars aren't even made in America anymore. Nothing is.

Nannu had already renounced his last name in favor of melting-pot anonymity. He told me once, slouching in the doorway to the kitchen, that Ellis Island had that effect on a lot of people back then.

I've called my grandfather Nannu ever since I was a kid. It doesn't do justice to how fierce he was. He came to Boston from the old country, before the war. Some people hated Greeks back then. Nannu struggled to feed his family, since no one wanted to hire him. Grandma's family wouldn't help either. Being Irish, they were in a better position—they had been here longer. But they never approved of Nannu, who would take any work he could find—construction and carpentry, mostly. Sometimes cleaning toilets. He never made much of himself, at least compared to Henry Ford, but those of us who loved him felt differently.

"Breakfast, Ford!"

"Down in a sec!" I yell back.

I hear Boston in my voice. People notice my accent when I'm caught off guard, irritated, or half asleep, like I am now. I carefully trained myself to be rid of it. Now I speak a perfect California tongue, flavorless as tap water. Here in Sacramento, people converse with perfectly blended uniformity, as similar as the pastel tract homes we live in.

I lumber down the stairs to see Mom sipping a latte.

"Morning, honey," she says, holding a cell phone away from her ear. She stuffs papers into her briefcase with lightning speed. A mass of hair, recently bleached, frames her olive features.

I nod and grab breakfast. The toast is a little burnt, and all the windows are open to prevent the smoke alarm from screaming bloody murder. I smear apricot jam over the blackened square. It's pretty much inedible, so I throw a banana in my backpack for later.

Mom says "uh-huh" into her phone several times and pulls it away to say, "You look tired. Sleep OK?"

I nod.

She gets back to her call. "No, I'm listening," she says. "See you then." She hangs up. "Well"—she kisses my cheek—"I'm off." She gives me the once-over. "Is that what you're wearing to school?" She takes the last swig of her latte and blots her lipstick with a tissue.

"Yeah." I look down at my T-shirt and track pants. Everyone at school wears "ghetto." It's the "in" thing. "Why not?"

"Nothing." She checks her watch. "Would you get my dry cleaning on the way home? I have a client tomorrow."

I nod. I don't know Mom anymore. As soon as we moved west after the divorce, she landed her job at the ad agency and bought all new clothes. "For a new me," she had declared after a trip to Talbots. She's become like those women I used to make fun of at the mall. Gone is the Boston Mom who'd shop at thrift stores and make roast lamb. Now it's all about gourmet coffee, and she even wears blazers on the weekend. Linen, she assured me, *is* casual.

"See you tonight, then." She kisses my forehead.

"Yeah, see ya," I reply.

Going with Mom after the divorce was like my own Ellis Island. It was hard to leave Dad; the look on his face when we drove away made my gut sink. I felt like a traitor. Now our regular summer visits—his part of the custody agreement—are pretty strained. He dates now, women with names like Amber and Kim. He slugs my arm and asks if I'm trying out for any sports teams. We eat burgers and

fries and channel-surf. I love him and all, but jeez—
Mom was headed to California!

I stand in the quad between fifth and sixth periods.
She passes by me on the way to her locker, and I purr
her name, a nearly audible whisper. *Helena.* She is my
dream woman, though she doesn't know that I exist.

Helena's a junior, a year ahead of me. She's not a
popular cheerleader, nor is she in Math Club—she's
without categorization. She doesn't stand out; she's
neither popular nor unpopular, and she isn't noticed
for being either perfect or flawed. I guess you'd call
her "average." She's as American as apple pie; *she*
could be named after a car manufacturer.

Helena gets a book from her locker and continues
down the hall, her black curls trailing behind her
wickedly. Like snakes that keep watching me.
Tempting me.

Ford, she beckons dreamily, soft and distant. *I
want you.*

I head to the bathroom before sixth period and
catch myself in the mirror.

Not again.

I try to avoid my reflection—I want not to look—but a corner, a fragment of my image, sucks me in. I step back and examine the picture. I look like an olive blob. I move closer, my nose near the glass, and focus. I stretch out my face with my palms and search for zits. I examine every pore before moving on to the hair check. Not the hair on my head—I mean a *real* hair check. My eyebrow—that is to say, my unibrow—looks particularly bushy. Almost Neanderthal. I could be a caveman for Halloween. I wouldn't even need a costume.

I need to pluck or shave in between my eyebrows; that much the mirror tells me. The mirror tells me many things, like an honest friend who ought to shut up once in a while. Chest hair is creeping from under my T-shirt like a fungus—I need to trim that, too. Maybe I should start wearing button-down oxfords, buttoned all the way to my Adam's apple. I could push my tuft down and conceal it.

A toilet flushes and I freeze. I am not alone. I try to act cool, checking my hair—the ones on my head.

138

Nothing weird about that, all the guys do it between classes. I grab the comb from my back pocket and get started. A stall door opens and Jason Keller walks out.

"Checking for ticks, Ape?"

I ignore him, pretending to be preoccupied.

He stands behind me and makes monkey sounds. "Eee-ee!! Ooo-oo!!" Then he screeches.

"Shut up," I say. "Leave me alone." I wipe my bangs from my eyes and see hair on my knuckles. On my knuckles! I am a caveman. I should drag my hands on the ground as I walk.

Jason keeps making monkey noises. "Eee-ee!! Ooo-oo!!" He scratches under his armpits, like a primate.

I fling open the bathroom door and scramble outside. I feel stupid and vain, like I'm some pretty boy, which I'm not. Pretty boys care about this stuff, not real guys with depth and character. Or do they? Can you have depth while still caring about the surface?

I sit in the quad after sixth period, eating my banana, when the symbolism suddenly hits me. I dash to the garbage can and throw it away before anyone sees. That would be a real winner for the yearbook—part of the geeks-and-losers pictorial. I sit again and wait, ignoring my growling stomach. I know she will come.

Almost on cue, Helena cuts through the crowd. I sit back and watch, like a voyeur. I wish that I could participate in my own life—that I could speak to her. Maybe write her a letter. Instead, I feel like I'm watching a dumb movie.

Helena walks to her locker. She's alone, another sign we'd be perfect together. Neither of us would have to be alone anymore. I wonder if she spends all her time in her room, like I do. I wonder if she also has no one to talk to. She dials her combo, flips the latch, and rummages through her locker. She radiates light. I want to touch her. I imagine her dark curls caressing my face like tiny fingers as she kisses me. I catch her scent on the wind—she hints of pear. Or maybe apple. My facial muscles stretch into smiling . . .

Look over here! my smile says from across the quad. I send her a psychic transmission. A mental

S.O.S. *Notice me. Over here. I may be hairy, but I think I love you.*

She grabs her algebra book and gently slams her locker. "Gently" and "slams" is a weird way to think about it, but she even slams her locker with grace and dignity. She's just amazing.

She never even looks in my direction.

She never sees the Ape.

Sitting on my bed after school, I mull over the day's events. Stupid Jason Keller and his monkey sounds. Beautiful Helena not knowing that I exist. Something has to give. I think about her every night before going to bed. I obsess over a girl who doesn't even know my name, and it makes me feel sick inside. Need is a powerful thing—it makes your gut feel hollow like a drum and can hurt as it pounds loudly in your ears.

I look at the photo of Nannu on the bureau next to the mirror. Nannu used to tell me stories of bar fights he had been in—to let off steam—and how winning would always lead to a tattoo. They were like badges of courage, testaments to his strength, and each one had a story. His arms were covered in ink; he could never fully hide them. No matter which shirt he'd wear, waves and snakes always traveled beyond what could be concealed.

My favorite was the heart he got for Grandma. She refused to get a matching one. "Proper women don't get tattoos," she once told me. I suspected it was hard enough for her family that she married a Greek, without her getting inked. Still, she'd always show off Nannu's with great pride to anyone who'd look. "See?" she'd ask, pointing. "It says *Emma*."

The summer I was twelve, Nannu gave me some advice I've never forgotten. One day he and I were in the kitchen as Grandma made sandwiches.

"Can I have a kiss?" Nannu asked her.

She smiled, wiped her hands on her apron, and pecked him on the lips.

"Ford," he said, smiling, "never be afraid to ask for what you need."

Nannu knew about need. The way he fed his family through his sacrifices proved that much. His words had stayed with me years after my Nannu went to his grave. It was another legacy, in a way.

I pull a pencil from my bag. *No, I think, use pen. You can't take it back that way.*

> *Dear Helena,*
> *You don't know me, but I wish you did. I think about you all the time and wish I could talk to you. There's so much I feel—I need you to know—but it would come out wrong if I tried to tell you. Maybe someday we'll meet and you'll see I'm not who people say I am.*

I leave it unsigned. Without my name, she can't track me down, so there's nothing to lose.

The next day after fifth period, I stand in the quad. I study the note in my hand, wondering if I should go through with it. I walk down the hall with forced ease, passing her locker on the right side. She is bent over, looking for her sixth-period algebra book. Her butt looks like a small candy heart; I practically lose my breath. I could gaze at her bending over this way forever, but instead I slip the note into the pack slung over her shoulder and keep walking, unseen.

Nothing changes. The next day between classes, I watch her for signs. She doesn't look around quizzically, searching faces for clues, searching for her anonymous love. She doesn't smile secretively; she doesn't hum or giggle or walk with a slight bounce. Maybe the note wasn't enough to inspire that kind of reaction?

Seeing her smile with the knowledge that someone cared for her would have filled me up. I think it would have been enough to keep me going. Perhaps the note got stuck in a folder, or maybe it was still in her pack, under a textbook? I bet she never even read it.

I wait a few days, monitoring her behavior like an anthropologist, but Helena is "business as usual." As if nothing had happened.

In bed at night, I still see her face as I drift off to dream. She stands by her locker in a black dress, her curls cascading down her tender back. She starts to speak, but Nannu's scratchy voice comes out of her supple mouth. *Ford,* she says, *never be afraid to ask for what you need.*

I wake in the morning with Helena's image and Nannu's voice both still in my head. It's an upsetting combo, a real killjoy to be sure, and there's only one way to make his voice stop.

I have to follow his advice precisely. I have to ask for what I need. But how can I ask for something when I don't know what it is? *At least give it a shot, Ford,* I tell myself.

I shower, towel off, and put on a shirt I got for Christmas—a baby blue oxford. I approach the mirror with my eyes closed. I don't want to do it this time. I want to look objectively. No harsh criticisms, no judgment. I run a comb through my hair and try to find the positive. My blue eyes are the first thing I notice; the shirt brings them out. In a good way. My hair is parted and looks clean. Girls like clean hair. I check my teeth and practice smiling—they are a little crooked. *Not any more than anyone else's,* I assure myself.

I practice smiling a few more times: the surprised, caught-off-guard smile; the spontaneous, devil-may-care smile; the alluring, come-hither smile. I want to be prepared for anything. And I want my smile to be ready.

I look at my ears and notice two black hairs. I can't help myself—I grab the tweezers and pluck them by the roots. It's hard to check the ear canal for hair, but my finger doesn't feel anything spiky. I picture myself as an old man with long gray hairs growing out of my ears. *It doesn't matter when you're seventy,* I think. *No one cares then.*

I check my eyebrows. Still bushy.

The unibrow has to go.

I grab the tweezers and pluck a few hairs from the middle. My skin stings and my eyes water. The tears start my nose flowing, so I blow into a wad of toilet paper. I snatch the tweezers again and pull a few more hairs. Each pluck feels like a tiny bee sting. My eyes stream and turn bloodshot. It looks as though I've been crying. Plucking is a slow process. At this rate, I'll be yanking away until second period.

I clutch my razor and hold it to the middle of my eyebrow, where I'd already started weeding. I run the razor down the middle, and a huge patch is mowed.

But it doesn't look even.

I stand back and try to figure out which eyebrow is OK and which is too short. Or maybe one's too long? The left one—right, I guess, in the mirror— looks like it could be shorter. I shave a tiny fraction off it and stand back. It still looks crooked, but I can't figure out why. The shape is wrong, I think. The right one—wait, that's left—should be rounder and not so flat. I angle the razor, the corner against the tip of the brow. I try to carve a shape, but accidentally carve more than I bargained for. I nick a bump, a zit maybe, and draw blood. It bleeds a lot. I press toilet paper on the bump and hold it until it stops. It looks like a wasp sting. I use some of Mom's makeup to hide the redness.

I stand back to assess the damage. I look weird; having two discrete eyebrows makes my face look balanced, if perpetually surprised. And the makeup looks obvious. I grab a baseball hat and pull it down close to my eyes. I've seen lots of guys at school do this, so I figure I'm safe. My red eyes should clear by the time I get to school.

I head toward the back door in the kitchen. Mom is drinking her morning latte from the machine. "Honey, would you make yourself something for dinner?" she asks, staring down at some papers. "I have a date tonight."

I avoid looking at her. "No problem."

"Chad and I are going for sushi."

Figures. It would be a Chad or a Steve, to rival Dad's Kim or Amber.

"Have fun," I say as I head out the door. I pass the picture of Nannu on the hall table. It is his wedding day, and he is dressed in a suit and tie. You can still see the tattoos, faint under his thin white shirt.

Mom always says how dapper he looks in this picture. "He looks like a real gentleman."

I wait by Helena's locker. I will speak my mind, until it is clear. I will make Nannu proud. She appears and our eyes meet.

"Hello," she says.

I open my mouth, but nothing comes out.

"Sorry," she says. "I need to get into my locker."
She smiles.

I move aside, mute.

I can't breathe. It feels like something is sitting on
my chest, but somehow I manage, "Hello, Helena." I
take a breath. "You don't know me, but I wish you
did." I've practiced this moment in the mirror count-
less times. I know the speech by heart.

Her face ignites with recognition. She interrupts
me. "*You* wrote that note!"

I stare at her, my mouth hanging open. Then I
nod.

"*Ape?*" she asks.

I stare at my hands. My hairy paws.

My heart races, the sound throbbing in my ears
like a drum being beat over and over. "My name is
Ford, not Ape," I say. "I'm not who people say I am."

She examines my face. "What happened to your
eyes?"

I look away and pull my baseball cap down farther.

"Your note," she says in a low voice. "It was sweet."

I gaze at her, hopeful, waiting.

Her eyes meet mine. She smiles. "But . . . you're not really my *type*."

My face begins to sweat, stinging my shaved eyebrows. "I can change," I say.

She shakes her head and heads down the hall.

I followed Nannu's advice to the letter, and it failed. I asked for what I needed, yet here I am. Looking at me, all she saw was *the Ape*. I don't blame her. It's all I see looking in the mirror, too. How can I expect her to see something I don't?

I stretch out on top of the already-made covers before breakfast. I look at the mirror on the bureau and see an ape-faced boy. Sick of my own image, I go downstairs, grab an apple, and head toward the door. Nannu's wedding picture makes me hesitate before leaving. He *does* look sophisticated.

He may have cleaned toilets and gotten into bar fights. He may never have amounted to much in

America. Maybe people hated him because he was Greek. But one woman—Grandma—saw past all of that. Nannu cleaned up well. Sure, you could see the tattoos through his shirt, and maybe his face was craggy—but still, he looked pretty smooth in his old fedora. I can see why Mom describes him as "a real gentleman." Sure, we could have been carnies at a sideshow together: *Ford, the Ape-Faced Boy, and Nannu, the Tattooed Man—fifty cents for a gander!*

But Nannu was anything but "average."

I look at the mirror above his picture, then back to Nannu. I alternate between staring at myself and at him until the images blur together. It never occurred to me how much I look like him. Our eyes are virtually identical.

"I miss you, Nannu," I say, before heading out the door.

CHEEK-BONES

Ellen Wittlinger

Lucy sat squirming in the parked car outside the modeling agency while her mother, Linda, pushed the naturally blond locks her daughter had inherited out of Lucy's face, then fluffed the hair up with her fingers. Manicured, pedicured, and dressed in tight jeans and a pink silk blouse, Lucy felt she'd been refurbished quite enough; besides, all this grooming was making her nervous. When Linda pulled the silver tube from her purse, Lucy rebelled.

"Get that stuff away from me!" she said, knocking

her mother's lipstick-wielding hand aside. "It's way too dark—I'll look like Lolita."

"You need some color in your face," her mother said, but reluctantly capped the tube.

"I have plenty of color," Lucy said. "You got me with that copper blush junk."

"It brings out your beautiful cheekbones." Linda continued to fuss with Lucy's long hair, which, released from the usual braids, fell in waves around her face. "I don't know why the boys aren't flocking around you," she said.

"Why would I want boys to flock around me?"

"It's those silly braids you insist on wearing to school," Linda continued. "And why you wear glasses when you have contact lenses, I'll never understand."

"OK, OK," Lucy threw open the car door and pulled herself out of her mother's clutches. "Let me get my cheekbones inside and get this over with."

"I've got your pictures," Linda said as she climbed out of the car on the driver's side, waving the black portfolio.

"You're coming in *with* me?" Lucy was appalled.

"I told you, honey, I know the office manager. Any little bit of pull might help you get signed. You never know."

Lucy stamped one foot in frustration. Her ankle, not used to being so far from the ground, turned slightly to the side. "Ow! Dammit! I hate these shoes!"

"And *please,* Lucy, try to act like a mature person when we get inside. They want you to *be* fourteen, but not to *act* fourteen."

How, Lucy thought, am I supposed to know how to act older than I am? I've never *been* older. "And how mature am I going to look if my *mommy* has to come inside with me?" she muttered.

Linda gave Lucy a big, excited smile as they entered the building. "Break a leg!" she said.

In the platform shoes Linda had forced her to wear, Lucy thought she probably *would* break a leg. The two of them climbed the stairs, and Lucy pulled open the door that said BACK BAY MODELING AGENCY. The reception room was all marble and chrome—white, silver, and shiny, like the hair salon her mother adored. Would she ever feel comfortable in places like this, Lucy wondered. This polished kind of environment seemed to be the required backdrop for women like her mother, whose personalities were as glossy as their lipstick.

"May I help you?" the receptionist asked, her eyelids barely able to hold up her heavy lashes.

"I guess I have an appointment," Lucy said.

"You *guess*?" the woman asked.

"She *does* have one," Linda said. "I'm her mother—and I'm a friend of Mary Crawford's, the office manager."

"Mary isn't here today," Heavy Lashes said. "Her dog got sick."

"Oh," Linda said, her shoulders drooping. "That's too bad."

The receptionist turned back to Lucy. "Name?"

"Lucy Furness."

"Furnace?" The woman paged lazily through a large book.

"Fur*ness*," Linda interrupted, pushing Lucy slightly to the side. "F-U-R-N-E-S-S."

"Here you are. You're seeing Hartwell. But we're kind of backed up this afternoon. Take a seat. I'll call you when he's ready for you." She pointed one long, lime green fingernail toward the waiting area, where a number of other females were already perched on the edges of bright red chairs, staring at the newcomers.

Lucy probably would have bolted right then, but Linda took hold of her elbow and steered her toward the seats. Linda said hello to the others in a polite but not particularly friendly way. Lucy smiled halfheartedly at the other girls while all of them sized up the competition.

Two of the girls seemed to be friends, or at least to have come together to the agency. They looked so alike, Lucy wondered if they were sisters; both had long dark hair, but one had unnatural red highlights running through hers, and the other wore dark red lipstick of the sort Lucy's mother had tried to force on her. When Lucy smiled, they put their heads together and whispered to each other.

The other couple in the chairs, Lucy was happy to note, was another mother-and-daughter duo. At least she wasn't the only girl who had a parent hovering over her.

"Sarah, when you get in there, don't forget to stand up straight," the mother was advising. "You always slump."

Sarah, a strawberry blonde who looked like she hadn't had a good meal in a month, rolled her eyes and sucked in her already concave stomach.

"Get off my back," she said. "Go eat a doughnut."

Sarah's mother, who was two or three times the size of her daughter, pulled back as though she'd been slapped, which, in a way, she had.

All three of the other girls were very pretty, Lucy thought. But were they pretty enough? Were they pretty in the right way? Did they have that magic *something*—her mother called it "sparkle"—that would get them chosen for modeling jobs? Lucy had no idea if the others had it or if she had it or even if she'd know it if she saw it.

Linda, who'd been a model herself in her teens, thought Lucy had it, but Lucy suspected that a mother wasn't the best judge of something like that.

157

Besides, Lucy wasn't sure she wanted to sparkle. Of course, the money she could make modeling would be a huge help in paying for college, which was the reason her mother gave for pushing the idea. It had paid for business school for Linda, which, as Linda always reminded her, had paid for everything else after the divorce.

"Don't expect your father to pay for college," Linda had told her. "He's got his *new* family to spend all his money on."

When Lucy had suggested she might be able to get a different kind of job, Linda had shaken her head. "You'll never make as much at some burger joint as you can modeling. It's the best money a kid can make. Besides, when you're a model, people pay attention to you."

"I don't want people to pay attention to me," Lucy had said.

"You will," Linda had assured her. "Soon."

So there she was, a girl who had always tried her best to be invisible, applying for a job in which she would spend large amounts of time standing in front of cameras in revealing outfits. Trying to make people pay attention to her.

Katherine, her best friend, had been shocked. "You? A model?" she'd said, glancing over Lucy's standard school apparel: an olive green T-shirt stuffed into baggy pants from the Salvation Army, belted with a man's tie. Not to mention her ancient Teva sandals held together, barely, with silver duct tape.

"Not that you aren't pretty enough," Katherine had said. "You definitely are; if I looked like you, I'd be ecstatic. But, you aren't the model *type*. I mean, you wear *braids*."

"What's wrong with braids? Why does everybody have to look the same, anyway?"

"We don't all look the same, goofball. You look way better than most of us. Except you don't really want to, which is why I love you. But I don't think that's how models feel." Katherine had cleaned her glasses on the hem of her T-shirt. "Models are like those A-list girls who spend hours dressing themselves and working over their faces in front of a mirror. They're all about being noticed. That's not you."

"I know," Lucy had said. "But the money is so good. Maybe I could learn to sparkle while I'm there and still be the old me here. Like Superman and Clark Kent."

"Maybe," Katherine had said doubtfully. "But right now you're the antisparkle."

Lucy was jostled from her daydreams by the banging of the door. Everyone in the waiting area turned to stare at the woman who had just entered the room on six-inch heels, her frosty hair swinging around her broad, tan shoulders, a miniskirt grazing her muscled thighs.

The receptionist managed to pry open her heavy lids. "Celia! You're here! They're waiting for you in back!"

"Is Kent here?" the model said. "I won't have anyone else touch my hair. You know that."

"He's here. Go on back."

Celia patted her own hair as though it were a beloved animal. "The last time, that awful woman *ruined* me. I'm not even going in there if Kent isn't here."

"He's *here*," the receptionist repeated. "And they're waiting."

"He better be," Celia said. She turned briefly to flash her eyes over the girls in the waiting area, wrinkled her lip, and walked off down the hallway.

"That was *Celia Johnson*," Sarah whispered to no one in particular.

Red Highlights nodded. "I know. She's the highest-paid model at this agency."

"I worked with her once," Red Lipstick said, tossing her hair.

"You *did*?" Sarah's eyes narrowed.

"Yeah, when you were a baby!" Red Highlights said.

"No, I was seven! It was a back-to-school layout for Macy's. She was supposed to be a teenager, but she was already at least twenty."

Highlights nodded. "She must be in her late twenties by now. Can't last much longer."

"Yeah, get out of the way, Celia! Here we come!" Lipstick laughed.

Linda poked Lucy in the side. "That's why you start doing this young. You're lucky if your career lasts until you're thirty. I was finished by twenty-five."

"I don't *want* to do this until I'm thirty," Lucy said. "I just want to make money for college."

Sarah and the sisters stared at her. "Not a good attitude," Sarah said. "Don't let *them* hear you talk that way. Although, I shouldn't tell you that. If you hang yourself, there's a better chance for me. Especially since we're both blondes."

If Lucy *hanged* herself? Nice. Were these the people she'd be working with if she started modeling? Girls who hoped you'd hang yourself so they'd have a better chance? Women like Celia who thought they were royalty just because they were shaped like coat hangers? She couldn't wait.

Her mother patted Lucy's knee and leaned over to whisper, "Don't let them get you rattled. They're just scared because you're the prettiest girl here."

They were scared of *her*? That was just ridiculous.

After a few more minutes both Sarah and the look-alikes were called to the back. Lucy waited with the two mothers.

"Has Sarah done much modeling?" Linda asked Sarah's mother.

"Some, yes," the mother answered. "But not as much as she'd like. She's quite ambitious. How about your daughter?"

Linda smiled serenely. "She's just getting started. But I'm sure she'll do well. I modeled for many years and got so much out of it. Not just financially, either. I made lots of friends, and I actually met my husband through modeling. He's a photographer."

"Really?" Sarah's mother seemed fascinated. She looked down at her own large dress sadly. "I was never the right size for modeling, but it looks like fun."

"Oh, it is," Linda assured her. "I loved it."

What? First of all, that wonderful photographer had walked out on them when Lucy was only four; Linda normally didn't have a good word to say about him. Lucy couldn't remember ever meeting any of her mother's other modeling "friends." And Linda had always said that modeling hours were long and tiring—it was a job, and never as much fun as you might think. So why was she giving this woman a snow job? Maybe this was what Linda liked about modeling—impressing people who thought being a model meant you were some kind of a celebrity.

"Lucy Furnace, you can go in now," the receptionist said. "Hartwell is ready for you. Room Six." The green nail pointed the way.

"Knock 'em dead!" Linda said, handing over the portfolio.

Lucy walked down the long hallway and opened the door to Room Six. It was a large room with a desk in one corner and a rack full of clothes in another. One wall was all mirrors. There was a man seated behind the desk who she imagined must be Hartwell, though whether that was his first name or last, she didn't know.

"Mr. Hartwell?"

He looked up, his eyes immediately taking her in—face, shoulders, breasts, waist, hips, legs, feet. She felt he was *absorbing* her.

"Just Hartwell is fine," he said. "Sit down, please." He motioned Lucy to a chair that was set off by itself about six or seven feet away from his desk.

Lucy sat down, her back rigid, her legs held tightly together.

Hartwell got up from his desk and paced around her. "Relax, Blondie. You're not at Lady Astor's tea party. Are those your pictures?"

"Oh, yes," Lucy said, handing them over.

Hartwell flipped through the pages, making little murmuring sounds. He squinted at Lucy. "You've got Sarah Jessica Parker's hair, lucky girl—it frames those dynamite cheekbones."

No, Lucy thought, I've got my *own* hair. And why did everybody care so damn much about cheekbones, anyway?

Hartwell was motioning to her to stand up, so she did. "How tall?" he asked.

"Um, five feet, eight inches."

"Weight?"

"About one-fifteen."

He peered up at her. "Not anorexic, are you?"

"No."

He snorted. "Like you'd tell me anyway."

"I'm not," Lucy said. "I've always been skinny. I eat a lot. I eat—"

"Whatever." Hartwell motioned for her to turn in a circle. "Measurements?"

"Thirty-two, twenty-five, thirty-four," she said, shifting nervously from one foot to the other. She hated having to tell personal stuff like this to a man. He wasn't even a doctor.

Hartwell looked straight at her breasts. "A-cup?"

"Uh, yeah."

"So a size-zero dress, then?"

Lucy shrugged. "I don't know. I don't wear dresses very often." Like, never. And anyway, what kind of a size was *zero*?

"Well, blouses, skirts . . . You wear *clothes,* don't you?"

"I . . . yeah. I guess I might be a size two." What difference did it make? When she bought clothes at the Salvation Army, she just got things she liked. She didn't really look at the sizes—if they were too big, she wore a belt.

"Shoes?"

Lucy was puzzled. "Yes, I wear shoes."

Hartwell looked as though she was trying his patience. "What *size*?"

"Oh, right. Eight and a half."

"Eyes?"

She wanted very much to say "two," but refrained. "Green," she told him.

He made a few marks on a piece of paper, then strode to the clothing rack and pulled a few items from their hangers. "Put these on and let me see how they hang," he said.

Lucy took the clothing and looked around for a changing room. "Where?"

"You're s*hy*?" Hartwell asked. He seemed surprised, as though he couldn't imagine anyone not wanting to strip to their underwear in front of him. "I'll turn my back."

Quickly Lucy slipped off her blouse and jeans and pulled on the short skirt and skimpy top he'd handed her. "OK," she said.

Hartwell turned around and surveyed her as though she were an inanimate object, yanking on the hem of the skirt, pulling the strap of the shirt down over her shoulder.

He stared at her rear end and said, "You've got kind of a devilish-angel thing going on. I might be able to make you hot."

A shiver ran through Lucy's body, and she put the strap back up in place.

"What are you doing?" he asked.

"It wasn't comfortable like that," she said. "It felt like it was falling off."

"Modeling is not about comfort, dear." He yanked the strap back down.

Lucy pulled it back up, then turned to face him.

"Do you have a problem?" he said.

"Yeah. I don't like you adjusting my clothes like that. Or staring at my butt, either."

Hartwell smiled as though he'd rather be poking out her eyes. "Well then, honey, maybe you wouldn't like being a model."

"I *wouldn't* like being a model," Lucy said. And she knew as soon as she said it that she wouldn't be a model, no matter what her mother wanted. Nobody was going to treat her like a poodle at a dog show. Forget it.

Hartwell seemed amazed. Apparently he thought everyone wanted to see themselves in *The Boston Globe* wearing slingbacks and a tankini.

"What?"

"You heard me. I think modeling is dumb."

Finally he stammered, "Well . . . but, you . . . you're here!"

"My mother used to model—she thought I should too. And I need to earn money for college, and there aren't many jobs you can do when you're fourteen. But I don't like people looking at me all the time. I can't do it."

Hartwell nodded. "Well, I can see why your mother wanted you to come; you certainly look like you ought to be a model."

"Maybe right now I do. But not usually. I don't like to dress up. Or wear makeup or contacts. Or have my hair flying around my face like this. I usually wear it in braids."

"You do, huh?" Hartwell stared at her another

169

minute and then smiled for real. "So, you honestly don't want to be a model?"

Lucy shook her head. "I think I would rather dig graves, or be the person who holds the Stop sign in the middle of the street when it's a hundred degrees out and they're tarring the road." She'd done it now. Lucy could just imagine the look on her mother's face when she told her she'd sabotaged the audition. Fur would fly.

"My God," Hartwell said. "I didn't think they *made* girls like you."

Her mother was talking on her cell phone when Lucy came out of the office. She hung up immediately and looked at Lucy expectantly.

"So? What happened?"

Lucy took a deep breath. "Well, I got a job," she said.

Linda's eyes got huge. "*Already?* They took you on and got you a modeling job in the same day? I've never heard of that. When I started—"

"It's not a modeling job, Mom," Lucy said. "I'm going to be a gofer on the weekends they do shoots."

Her mother stared at her, the grin on her face slowly subsiding into a jowly frown.

Lucy kept talking. "It's not like the animal, gopher. It means I'm the one who has to 'go for' things. I do stuff like make coffee, pick up lunches, move things around—"

"I know what a gofer is," her mother said. "You weren't applying for the job of *gofer*."

Linda threw the cell phone into her purse and stood up. "Let's get out of here."

Lucy followed her mother down the stairs. "It's a better job for me, Mom. I won't make as much as I would modeling, but I'll probably get more hours. And I'll learn some stuff about photography, too."

"Since when do you care about photography?"

"I'm only fourteen! I don't know what I care about yet!"

"You think you can be a photographer just because your father is?"

"No, that's not why . . ." But her mother had slammed through the door at the bottom of the stairs and was stalking across the sidewalk.

Once they were both in the car, Lucy tried again to explain. "Hartwell was glad I didn't want to be a model. He said everybody else who applies for any kind of job there *does,* and he's tired of dealing with all the wannabes. He said I can wear whatever I want—the worse I look, the better—because then the real models won't feel threatened by me."

Finally her mother spoke. "And that's what you want out of life? To be nonthreatening? Why did we waste our day in that agency if you don't want to be a model?"

Lucy shrugged. "I didn't know what it would be like. Once I got there and saw those other girls, and the way everybody treats you like a thing instead of a person, and how they're all jealous of each other . . . I didn't want to do it."

Linda shook her head, and they drove home in silence until, a block from their house, she said, "I can't believe you just threw over an opportunity like this. Most girls would kill for a chance like this."

"I'm not most girls. I'm me."

172

"I'm well aware of that," her mother said, spitting out the words.

The anger in the air was infecting Lucy now, too. "Well, who am I supposed to be? *You?*"

Her mother swung the car into the driveway and shoved the gearshift into park, then turned on her. "Don't you understand that this is for your own good? That I'm trying to help you?"

"How is getting my picture taken wearing a bunch of slutty clothing going to help me?"

"It will make you proud of yourself!"

Lucy almost laughed at that, but knew she'd better not. "No, it won't!"

"You'll learn how to dress, how to look your best. Then people will see you differently, see how beautiful you are."

"What people? Are we talking about *boys,* again?"

"Men like beautiful women—that's just how it works, Lucy, whether you like it or not. They want somebody with a little pizzazz!"

"Is that what Dad wanted?" Lucy knew it was a mean thing to say, but she was angry—and curious, too, whether her mother would be truthful. "Did you lose your *pizzazz*? Is that why he left you?"

Her mother's face slammed shut. "We aren't talking about your father."

"Well, maybe we should be. Why is it so important to you that I show off my hair and my legs and my stupid cheekbones? Just because you did? You act like my looks are the only valuable thing about me. Why do you want me to attract a bunch of shallow jerks who just want to go out with *models*? Did that work out for you?"

Her mother stared at her for a second, then looked away. "That's not what I'm saying, Lucy." But the anger had been swept from her voice.

Tears had started to gather in Lucy's eyes as the truth became obvious. "I don't want somebody to notice me for the way I look! I want them to notice *me*. The deep-down *me*! I don't want a boy who's going to leave me as soon as somebody prettier comes along!"

The way Dad left you. The words hung in the air between them, but Lucy didn't say them out loud. She didn't need to. Her mother closed her eyes and let her head fall back onto the headrest while Lucy swiped her arm across her face, taking off what makeup remained.

"The world can be hard for a woman," her mother whispered. "I only want to help you." Which Lucy believed was the truth.

"Don't worry," Lucy said. "What happened to you is not going to happen to me." She opened the car door and got out. As she walked across the lawn to the front door, she took off the uncomfortable shoes and let her bare feet dance through the tall grass.

175

On Saturday morning, Lucy woke up early. There was a shoot downtown at noon, her first paying job, but before that she had an appointment, and her mother had agreed to drive her.

The hairdresser swooned over Lucy's long, pale hair. "You just want the ends trimmed, right?" she asked.

"Nope. I want you to cut it short—very short. The kind of hairdo that doesn't even need to be combed."

"Really?" The woman sighed and bit her lip. "I'm afraid you'll regret it."

"Not a chance," Lucy assured her.

Soon, yellowy locks littered the floor. "I would have killed for hair like this at your age," the hairdresser said sadly.

"Yeah, but I'd just as soon not be murdered for my hair," Lucy told her.

When the woman finished up, Lucy put on her glasses and looked in the mirror. She ran her hand through the multilayered thicket. It felt good, and she decided it looked right—right for Lucy Furness. It was time for the change; she wasn't in grade school anymore, but she didn't intend to be a bimbo stereotype, either. Without the creamy, dreamy hair surrounding her head, it was clear she was nobody's devilish angel. This was the hairdo of a young woman with a responsible job.

This haircut said, I'm more than you think you see. Look carefully. Blondes can be smart, and smart girls can have cheekbones.

BINGO

Anita Riggio

I

I just wanted to see.

I only wanted to get to the very edge and look back at what I could leave, what I would leave. As if it mattered to anybody.

I remember beer cans. A pile of them in a clump of grass, glinting in the headlights.

And shards of silver slicing the river, cool and solid as swords.

Something skimmed my forearm. A carp? A trout? Sleeping with the fishes.

Maeve always laughed when some doughnut-nosed movie tough guy made remarks about sleeping with the fishes.

Then, black water . . . the tug of current—come along, come along—and beautiful, blessed silence.

So this is what it's like to die . . .

Until the thrashing—an arm under my chin. Drew's voice close to my ear—"Jesus. Jesus"—and him pulling me onto the bank, both of us coughing, sputtering. Then I heard Drew sobbing, saying, "You are messed up, Roscoe! Man, you are messed up . . ."

I opened my eyes then, looked straight up into the crown of that huge swamp maple, beyond the silhouette of black branches and leaves, to the stars.

I'd almost done it.

Jesus. God. I'd almost done it.

II

"So, you and Drew put the kayaks in the water yet?"

"Nah."

"How come?"

"I dunno."

"You gonna get them in the water soon?"

"Maybe."

Maeve and I were walking side by side down the lane toward the river. I didn't get how she wasn't afraid of me, of *It*, especially when everybody else—including me—seemed to be.

"Can I ask you something, Roscoe?" Maeve said.

"Probably not."

"What were you thinking?"

"What was I thinking when?"

"That night at the river. Did you really want to die, or did you just not want to deal?"

"Christ . . ."

"I mean, come on, Roscoe. You couldn't have thought that you could just check out being dead and then decide, no thanks, catch you later."

"I *didn't* think, OK? I just did it. Jesus, Maeve. Does everything that comes into your head have to come out your mouth?"

"Yup. Most of the time. Oh, look!" Maeve stood perfectly still, one arm outstretched, the other hand shielding the delight in her eyes. "The pair of cardinals. They could be oracles, you know."

I picked a long blade of reedy grass, glancing in the direction Maeve pointed. "Oracles, huh?"

"Yup. Frank and Til, my grandparents. Got to be." She laughed. "That male is one cocky little guy."

"Uh-huh." I walked away before she spun out on all that spiritual energy crap.

Maeve caught up, snatching a crab apple from a low-hanging branch. "You know you choose this, Roscoe," she said.

"Choose what?"

"You choose to stay closed off."

"Who'd you hear that from—an oracle?"

"We only ever get two choices: deal or don't. There's help for depression. Therapy and meds. Or herbs. Acupuncture, even—"

"Give it a rest, OK?" I grabbed Maeve's crab apple and pitched it at the heads of some cattails. "Don't you get on my case now, too. I'm fine. All right? Everything is just peachy."

Maeve didn't flinch. "You ever figure what this is costing you, Roscoe?"

I kicked a pebble; I had to kick something. If Drew had tried to ask this stuff, I might have kicked him. "Uh, I dunno. Maybe a buck fifty?"

She gave me the raised eyebrow while she decided whether or not to advance the troops. "Nice. Boy, you just keep that up."

We continued side by side down the path.

"Hey." Maeve flicked my arm. "I have an idea. How about we play bingo?"

"You have sincerely been hanging out at that church too much."

"Not that kind of bingo." She shoved a mass of dark curls away from her face. "I read it in a magazine. This would be 'Bingo for the Soul.' "

"And you have been reading those sappy self-help 'Soup' books again, too, I can tell."

Maeve downshifted to tank mode. "We make two bingo boards—one for you, one for me—and fill in the little squares with stuff that annoys us. Like in the cafeteria, for example, when you set down your tray and the entire table shuts up."

I stopped. "You making fun of me now?"

"Absolutely." Maeve bumped me with her hip. "C'mon. It's a coping strategy. Let's see . . . what else annoys Peter Roscoe?"

I started walking again.

Maeve bulldozed ahead, oblivious. "We could include a square for that Dina girl in chorus, who's always asking you, 'So, how are you, Peter?'"

"Man, she is so annoying . . ."

"Yeah. See? And—"

"Minelli, who asks me right in front of everybody, do I need more time for my take-home exam."

"Right!"

Our two shadows stretched out over the bumpy gravel path. Maeve was nearly skipping over mine.

"There should be a square for my mom, who sighs every time she looks at me," I said.

"OK. A square for your mother. Good." Maeve stopped, feet rooted, hands planted on her hips. "So, the first one to get bingo gets a prize."

"What's the prize?"

"I don't know. We'll have to work on that."

Her chin went up. She sniffed the air, turned, and found a fat cluster of honeysuckle. She put her face to it. "Mmm. Just smell this, Roscoe."

"I can smell it from here."

Maeve pulled a slim gold trumpet of a bloom from

the vine. "You can actually taste the honey, you know." She held it out to me.

"No thanks. I'm trying to quit."

"Ah, Roscoe," she said. "You just don't know what you're missing."

"Sure I do. You're keeping a running tally."

And I stood there with my hands in my pockets, watching Maeve take a hit off a honeysuckle blossom.

III

It rained so much in July and August that even the weather guys were complaining. I didn't care, though. I was spending serious hours in the basement watching Turner Classic Movies.

I like old movies. Nothing really hideous ever happens on-screen. You can depend on that. I saw *To Kill a Mockingbird* twice in one day. You've got to appreciate a dad like Atticus Finch. Not that I'm a big expert. Not that I ever had any kind of dad at all.

One afternoon, my mother set her green plastic laundry basket on the shag rug, perched at the edge of the futon, and watched Brando in *On the Waterfront* doing "I-coulda-been-a-contender." When they cut to a commercial, she sighed and started folding a load of my T-shirts. "Marlon Brando was so handsome when he was young . . . time changes everything, Peter," she said. "For bad and for good."

"Nice, Ma. Thanks."

She made a move to brush my cheek with the back of her hand, thought better of it, then hefted the laundry basket. She tried to sound casual when she suggested that I go out for a run or a walk or ice cream or air.

"You're going to get moldy down here, Peter," she said. I shrugged.

She sighed again and went on upstairs.

I wanted to tell her I was sorry for making her worry. I wanted to tell her I was sorry for acting like a jerk. Instead, I fished around between the cushions and found my bingo card.

Mom sighing. Square B-4. I made an X.

Drew came over one day during *This Property Is Condemned*. He planted himself and his basketball in front of the tube just as the mother showed up to haul Natalie Wood back to the boarding house.

"So, you plan on swimming this year, right?"

"I don't know."

"Roscoe. You're gonna quit the team?"

"You're in the way, Drew."

"What is up with you, man?"

"Nothing much."

"Roscoe, what are you doing?"

"Watching Natalie Wood. And you're still in the way."

Drew stood over me for a moment more. "This is bullshit . . ." he muttered, then took a seat on the futon.

He sprawled there, palming the basketball hard, one hand to the other. The slapping noise was annoying, rude even, and I wanted to holler at him, *Hey, have a little respect, would ya? Natalie Wood died, and now her little sister's got nothing left of her but one old dress and some stupid beads!*

I didn't holler, though. I just fingered my bingo card.

"What is wrong with you?" (All variations.) N-2.

Gestures of impatience, intolerance. O-5.

Whoo-boy. Two Xs. A bonus day.

When the final credits rolled, Drew stood up. "I'll see ya around, Roscoe," he said.

"Yeah. Later."

Drew didn't stop by after that.

Maeve came every afternoon after her babysitting job. She arrived at four twenty-five; you could set a watch by her. I clocked every sound from my barrel chair: the slam of her car door, the murmur of female voices in the kitchen, the scrape of a chair across the linoleum floor above my head, the click of the basement doorknob, the weariness in my mother's voice, "Peter, Maeve is here to see you." Then, the thunder of Maeve coming down the stairs, busting into my bunker.

"Hey" was all she'd say before she threw herself onto the futon. Sometimes I could hear Maeve swallowing unsaid words. Sometimes I could feel words rising up into my chest, but they never did make it out of my mouth.

All summer long, while Natalie Wood and Gregory Peck flickered on the dim screen in the basement, while I listened to footfalls on the floor above, the water trickling in the pipes, the washing machine chugging, the dryer whirring, and the voice in my head whispering, *You're worthless, Roscoe,* Maeve just sat beside me, twirling a strand of her hair and letting me be.

But one day early in August, Maeve stopped coming.

I didn't call her. Didn't see the point.

I figured even she had had enough.

IV

I overheard the news in the hallway, on the first day of school, from Dina and her stupid friend.

"So, you heard about Maeve?"

"What about her?"

"She has some kind of weird bone cancer."

"Omigod. Cancer?"

"That's what I heard."

"My grandmother died of cancer. Is Maeve's—like—fatal?"

"I don't know, but she wasn't in homeroom, and somebody said she's been in some big hospital in the city for two weeks."

"Wait. Remind me again. Who is Maeve?"

"She's the one with the really wild, curly black hair. She sang second soprano in chorus last year. She's supposed to be manager of the boys' swim team?"

"That sort of dumpy girl with the big mouth and the bigger laugh?"

"Yeah."

"Oh, I know who she is. That's too bad about the cancer . . ."

"Yeah. And it looks like the boys' swim team might need a new manager . . ."

"You are evil, Dina. You really are."

I bolted for the bathroom, slammed into a stall, and puked.

V

Maeve's mom dispatched the trick-or-treaters, then held out a full-size Hershey's bar to me. "Live it up, Peter," she said. "Maeve is in the family room."

"Bingo," Maeve said.

"No way. Let me see."

She pointed to the glass on the table and made a "gimme" gesture. I handed her the banana pineapple juice; she handed over her bingo board. "I do not lie." Maeve sipped her juice through the curly pink plastic straw I'd brought her. "The eyelashes did it. See?"

I scanned the card. G-4. Losing your eyelashes.

I glanced up at Maeve, still sipping. She batted her naked eyelids.

"OK," I said. "You win."

"Ha."

Maeve settled back on the half dozen Indian-print pillows behind her. The raspberry paisleys and turquoise curlicues looked too cheery against her shiny bald head. Three small beauty marks on her scalp made a tiny clover just above where her hairline had been. Patches of blue pooled in the hollows of her cheeks and on either side of her forehead.

If this had been a movie, there would have been violins—or a damn oboe, at least.

But this was no old movie.

Maeve unwrapped my Hershey's bar and broke off a piece. "So what's my prize, Roscoe?"

I looked at the bingo board in my hands. I shook my head. "I dunno."

"How about glitter nail polish?"

"Sure."

"Or a Snickers bar."

"Sure."

"Or a rhinestone butterfly hair clip."

"Sure."

She waited.

I glanced at her. If Maeve had had an eyebrow, she would have raised it.

"Ah shit, Maeve . . . I can't do this."

"Can't do what?"

"This. Play stupid bingo. Be with you. Sit here, while you—you—" I couldn't look at her.

"Jeez, Roscoe," she said quietly. "You've really got it rough."

"What?"

"Are you kidding me? Poor *you*?" She bolted upright. "Dammit! I sat with you all last summer while you were deciding whether or not to value the very thing I could be losing."

"You are not losing."

"I could be losing, Roscoe! I'm scared that I'm losing. I'm scared and I'm pissed off and I hate this and I hate that you refuse to see it. Would you just open your eyes? Look at me!"

"I am looking at you, Maeve."

"No! I mean, *see* me."

"I do see you. And I think—I think you're beautiful."

"Right." Maeve collapsed back on her pillows. She closed her eyes. After a long moment, she opened them and turned her head toward me. "So, just your luck, huh, Roscoe? To love a bald girl?"

I moved over to the hassock, lifted Maeve's bunny-slippered feet, and held them in my lap. "Yeah . . . just my luck to love a bald girl."

Maeve blinked. She fingered a strand of fringe on the prayer shawl some lady in church had made for her. "Yeah . . ." she said.

I tossed the cardboard then, and sent it sailing across the room like a Frisbee. "Time to make a new bingo board."

VI

Maeve died seven weeks later, more spirit than body.

I sat in the back of the funeral parlor for the duration of the wake: two to five and seven to ten. I stared at that closed casket and tried to fathom where all the life had gone that had been in the body now sealed in that shiny wood box.

Seems the entire high school processed up that aisle. People came who never even really knew Maeve. Dina bawled the whole time she was in the viewing line, and was sobbing so hard by the time she got to the front that some other girl had to sit her down and rub her back.

Drew showed. After he shook hands with Maeve's family, he came and sat with me for a while.

"Hey, Roscoe."

"Hey."

"This is tough, huh?"

"Yeah."

"Sorry, man. I mean, I know you two were tight."

I looked at him.

"I'm really sorry, man."

And Drew sat with me while I cried.

VII

I paddle slowly past the big swamp maple and listen to my oars dipping in and out of the river. A fat carp skims the surface, flipping his tail. When I spot a pair of cardinals, I pull up and listen to the cocky little male sing his cocky little song.

Later, when I walk up the lane from the river, I stop and press my face into a tangle of honeysuckle.

A feisty little honeybee lights on a nearby blossom. I nip off a flower, taste the sweetness.

And I think, *Bingo, Maeve. This one's for you.*

to Survive a

Norma Fox Mazer

1. In Seventh Grade at Mallory Central School

Mr. Giametti says, "I want you people to learn to love poetry and understand metaphors," and he reads us this poem:

> Music
> is a naked lady
> running mad
> through the pure night.

We seventh graders are not ready for this. Not in

Mallory, not in our small town on the Canadian border in the north of New York State that almost no one in the world has ever heard of.

Later that day, I find a note in my locker, which reads:

> Beauty H.
> is an old cabbage
> boiling mad
> on the pure stove.

I think this is pretty funny, and I even like the boiling mad part, especially because I know that people think I'm wussy, but inside me I'm not—only, that's not the point here. The point is, I'm about to show the poem to Gracie Pryor, who has the locker next to mine, but then I turn the paper over and see the drawing on the other side showing a girl with a head like a cabbage, and in case I don't get that it's meant to be me, there are the letters *B. H.* in a balloon with an arrow pointing to the drawing, and I just stand there, staring at the little drawing that, to tell the truth, does, in some weird way, look like me. *Cabbage head,* I think. *That's me. That's what I look like.*

2. IF I COULD BE ANYONE

I'd be a girl with a name that nobody would ever notice. I'd have a plain, ordinary name like Ruth Ford or Bea Stone or Lyn Smith, and I'd wear glasses, and my skirts a little too long and plain white blouses, and I would be an average student and sit in back of every class and be someone nobody ever noticed for any reason whatsoever. However, and I say this without any intention of boasting, I am not that average student. I have 20/20 vision, and like all the girls in our town of Mallory, I wear my skirts short, my blouses colorful, and my jeans tight.

Once I had a friend named Mary Jones, which is maybe the plainest of all names, but Mary Jones was somebody you would always notice. Mary Jones had straight, white-blond bangs hanging in her eyes and a tilt to her chin that made her look like a baby movie star. She lived out past the bus lines and threw dramatic tantrums whenever her mother was late picking her up, terrorized our teacher with more tantrums, and on the playground one day bit her middle finger and then mine, drawing blood to seal her promise that she would be my friend, and mine only, forever.

When she moved away in the middle of the year, I sorrowed for a month, which is a very long time for a seven-year-old. I never forgot my sorrow at Mary Jones's desertion, and that is exactly when I promised myself *I* would never break a promise.

3. THINK OF THIS

My parents, in a moment of insanity or, more kindly, misguided enthusiasm, named me Beauty.

Beauty Herbert. This is the name that I bear from year to year. Not even a middle name or initial to ease the oddness, the strangeness, the sheer wrongness of that name.

When I was little, it didn't matter. Little is a different time. As far as I have been able to determine, everyone thinks little kids are beautiful. I believe I am right in saying that.

Question: How many times do adults say, to even the ugliest of babies, "Oh, you little beauty"? I'll tell you how many times. Many. Many, many, many. Uncountable numbers of times. *Infinite* numbers of times.

But it is one thing to be an infant, ugly or otherwise, and be named Beauty, and it's quite another cuppa cocoa, as my mother likes to say, to be thirteen and so named.

You may take my word for it.

And if you think I'm making a fuss over nothing much, it's only because you have never been saddled with a name that people, and especially boys, find endlessly funny.

4. BOYS

Boys, boys, boys. Boys are *creatures.* Yes, I know we're all creatures, biologically speaking, but boys—boys are different creatures. I'm sorry if I'm being sexist about this, but they are. You know they are. They shove and jostle and grin with a lot of teeth showing, and they look at you if you're a girl and not gorgeous and hot and say mean things to your face. OK, not all boys. I know that's not all boys, but so many of them are that way—sort of mean and scary—but you know what, I still like them. I like boys, and I want one. I want a boy for myself. There is this one boy I see in school, and secretly I call him *my boy.* My boy has hair the color of dried-out grass, sort of brown gold.

My boy's eyes are that color, too, brown with gold bits. My boy plays baseball, and I'm on the girls' softball team, so we have something in common, although he doesn't know it. I'm not even sure he knows I'm alive, but I know he is, and I know his name, and whenever I see him, I think to myself, *There's my boy.*

5. WHAT I DO EVERY MORNING

Wake at 5 a.m. Tiptoe around my sisters, who snore and mutter and sleep on. Make my bed, wash, brush teeth and hair, pull on clothes, and look in the mirror no more than three times. Make breakfast for my little sisters, wake them up, herd them along to get dressed, check that Fancy, who's retarded—yes, she is, even if Mom and Dad insist on calling her slow—hasn't forgotten to put on underpants, make a pot of coffee for Mom, check if she has enough ciga-rettes to last the day, drink a glass of milk, find my books in the clutter, yell good-bye, and walk to school, dreaming, *Someday . . .*

6. SOMEDAY I WILL DO THESE THINGS

Live in a big city.

Rename myself.

Lose weight.

Learn not to giggle at the wrong times.

Become someone other than funny-looking Beauty Herbert.

7. NAMES

I keep a book of names, *acceptable* names, and add to it whenever a name settles in my mind and refuses to leave.

My four present favorites are Rebecca, Bethany, Joseanne, and Michelle. Previously, I had other favorites, including Wendy, Shawna, Krystal, Kelli, Jessie, and—oh, this is one I believe I will go back to—Victoria Rose.

8. MY PARENTS ARE CRAZY

I sorrow to say this, but yes, they are. Crazy. I know this is not a nice way to talk about your parents, but what is the use of being thirteen and nearly grown-up if you don't begin to think the things you want to think and say the things you want to say?

At the same time, you do not say these things to others if you live in Mallory, which is, I sorrow to say, the armpit of New York State.

In Mallory, if you are a girl, you are called upon to be nice, agreeable, and pleasant, but as yet there is no ban on saying the things you want to say *to yourself.*

So I have come to the point, to the very place, where I say everything to myself that I believe. If not to anyone else, then to myself.

So.

My parents are crazy. People have mental illnesses and they can't help it, but that does not include my parents. They are not mentally ill. They're just crazy nuts.

Blossom, darling, my father says in syrupy, adoring tones to my cigarette-smoking, sweaty-smelling, slow-moving mother. *H. H., you're always right,* my mother says in hoarse, sugary lilts to my love-handles-never-keeps-a-regular-job-Mr.-Fixit-fixes-everything-everywhere-but-in-his-own-home father.

"They say it's going to rain," my mother announces over her first cup of coffee. "They say we might get a tax increase. They say the schools aren't doing their job." She says the same three things every morning of every day, but still my father, Huddle, looks at her adoringly, as if she's spoken Truth from the Mount.

So.

Ignore my name, for the moment. Consider my father's name, Huddle Herbert. *Huddle* Herbert? Where did this name come from? I'll tell you where it came from. Not from his parents. They named him Herbert. Herbert Herbert. Do you see a pattern here? Already, in my grandparents' generation, names bear a sinister weight. Why would they name a child Herbert Herbert? Why not name him Bobby Herbert? Or Billy Herbert?

In any case, my father renamed himself, and only he knows from what strange tree he plucked the name Huddle. He says it was this name, though, that made my mother fall in love with him. This is quite possible.

Does any of this make my sisters' names, which are Mim, Faithful, Fancy, Autumn, Clarity, and Charity, reasonable names?

I think not. I say not.

Take my sister Mim. I have several theories on the subject of this name. What are they, you ask? I'll tell you. Theory #1: Still dizzy from the delirium of naming me, their first child, Beauty, and totally clueless, they searched for another equally awful name to give their next child. Theory #2: Since my sister was born small and skinny, they searched for a name they thought minimal. Theory #3: They thought it was a good joke.

Poor Mim. Hers, I sorrow to say, is a *crazy name.*

I do not know if Mim suffers from her name, as I do from mine, since she rarely speaks, unlike the rest of the Herbert family, who chatter-chatter-chatter endlessly.

Endlessly, I say.

I see that I am becoming very critical of my family, especially my parents, but also my sisters, who, after all, are innocent victims of my parents' foolishness.

Don't they say that this is normal for adolescents? Don't they say that the teen years are the time when you begin to criticize what you have always before accepted?

9. PROMISES TO MYSELF

I promise to chatter less.

I promise to eat less junk food.

I promise to smile less at stupid things I shouldn't smile at.

I promise never to smile when anyone says *how interesting* after hearing my name, or *that's different,* or *how weird,* or *how anything.*

I promise to try to keep my promises.

I promise not to hate myself if I can't keep all my promises all the time.

10. HOW TO SURVIVE A NAME

Stay small. When you are small, you are also ignorant. You don't think about your name *as a name.* Your name is like your toes or your belly button. It's just there. You think you were born with it.

Stay cute. When you are cute—and small—you do not realize that this is not a constant. Is not an unchanging state. Is not something that will never end.

Begin to understand this in first grade, when your front teeth fall out and your parents look at you and laugh. And laugh. And laugh. And your dad says, "Toothless Beauty." And your mom says, "Toothless Beauty," at which they both laugh and laugh and laugh.

Smile uncertainly. You are not sure what's going on, but you know it's something new.

Look at yourself in the mirror. Although you're only six years old, you will have a Moment of Truth. You will see your chubby, rough-skinned arms; your fat, crooked legs; your gaping smile.

Accept the news that descends on you. You. Are not. A beauty. You have the name, but not the game.

Forget the mirror. You don't care that much when you're six. Or seven. Or even eight. When you're nine, you can still manage a smile when the dentist gives you the once-over and then the twice-over and says with a snicker, "Your name is Beauty?"

Don't think too much about the tone that says as plain as cheese, *Beauty? You? Uh-uh! No way.*

After this, try not to think about your name at all. Especially after your twelfth birthday.

Remind yourself that your name is what it is, and you are not what your name says you are. You are not a beauty.

Remind yourself that this is all right.

Remind yourself that a name is just a name.

Remind yourself that when you are eighteen, you can change it.

Write this down: "When I am eighteen, I will change my name." Put the paper under your pillow. Look at it every night. Whisper those words to yourself.

If you still can't help brooding over your name, say it twenty-five times quickly.

Now laugh, because it's no longer a name, just a sound.

BELLA in Five ACTS

Tim Wynne-Jones

I

It was Tiny Rathbone who found Bella. He was in the auditorium, alone, he thought. He was working up a skit for the end-of-the-year talent show. Maury Kittel was going to play a fantasia for trombone; Tiffany Voltemand and Melissa Wong were doing interpretive dance. There were three comedy acts, four singer-songwriters, and five thrash bands. A bunch of jocks in drag were going to lip-synch to "Oops! . . . I Did It Again." Tiny wanted to do something a little different.

He was sitting on the lip of the stage, wearing a lime green bathing cap, a bright orange flotation device, a shiny blue swimsuit, and red water skis. The towline hung limply between his legs and snaked off into the front row, a yellow umbilical cord connecting him to the shadows.

He was making it up as he went along. The stage would be empty. The houselights would go to black. A hot special would come up directly overhead, and there he would be, watching the towline unwind.

"To be, or not to be, that is the question . . ."

Tiny's voice filled the auditorium. It was a high and mighty voice for such a diminutive creature, and he listened to it with pleasure until the darkness and the empty seats soaked up every last decibel. Then he heard a sound that was not his voice, a faint groaning sound. He looked around. The stage behind him was set for *My Fair Lady*. He was sitting in Professor Henry Higgins's book-lined study. The professor wasn't home.

He turned back toward the auditorium, straightened his arms, and slightly arched his back. He remembered to keep his tips up. Then he cleared his throat.

"Whether 'tis nobler in the mind to suffer
The slings and arrows of outrageous fortune
Or to take arms against a sea of troubles . . ."

He paused, let the towline fall. You couldn't start with *Hamlet*. Where did you go from there? He listened to the stillness, the distant hum of emptying halls. And then he heard it again, unmistakably a low groan.

"Hello?"

Nothing. He dropped the towline and worked his way out of the skis. He stood up, rubbing the circulation back into his ankles.

"Come out, come out, wherever you are!" he shouted. No one came out. Nothing stirred. A groan, he thought. A lightbulb went on under the lime green cap. The skit could start with a groan. Yes.

He would rise from the primordial ooze. He would borrow some reptilian costume from Tiffany Voltemand. There would be low, eerie lights and a murky reptilian sound track, and he would materialize somehow . . . from where?

The trapdoor. Perfect!

He marched upstage and heaved back Professor Higgins's threadbare carpet. There it was. Tiny had emerged from that very hole as Puck in *A Midsummer Night's Dream.* This time, however, he would emerge as some much-earlier life-form, something just learning how to breathe. He would slither out of the hole and crawl into his spotlight, blinking furiously. He would stand and strip— always a showstopper—and underneath his snake-skin he would be in his brave blue trunks. He would sit on the stage edge and put on his skis, and as he recited Hamlet's soliloquy, the music track would change from monks singing a Gregorian chant to Mozart to Beethoven and then jazz and Hitler and the atomic bomb going off and rock 'n' roll and Martin Luther King and Eminem and a Burger King commercial. He would water-ski across history—as much as he could squeeze into about four minutes.

What did it mean? Who knew? Who cared!

The tape would end with a CNN report from some war. No, better: The tape would end with the moment toward which all of history had been leading,

Mr. Scales coming on over the loudspeaker to remind everyone about the new dress code.

The crowd would go wild. He could already feel the warmth of their laughter. For one bright moment he wouldn't be tiny at all. Triumphantly, he hoisted open the trapdoor. And that's when he found Bella.

She was curled up like a fetus on a ratty mattress at the bottom of the hole. She groaned, and her arm tried unsuccessfully to reach up toward him but instead fell limply across her eyes.

Tiny jumped down and knelt at her side. Her beautiful face was deathly white and lying in a pool of vomit. An empty prescription drug container was stuck in the sick; a half-empty bottle of Evian water stood beyond the tangle of her golden hair. He grabbed the bottle and splashed her face. She startled and her eyes opened. Wide. Such wide, staring eyes.

I have seen that expression before, thought Tiny. Then her eyes closed and she stopped breathing. He doused her lips with the last of the Evian, and then, with a hand pressing lightly on her stomach, he bent down to give her the kiss of life.

"Hey, what's going on down there?"

Tiny glanced up. It was Horace, the custodian. "Call 911!" Tiny shouted, and returned heroically to his task. He was still at it when the ambulance arrived.

II

Tiny visited Bella in the hospital. He thought a lot about what to wear, deciding, finally, on the rabbit suit. The dog had chewed up one of the ears, and the fluffy tail was hanging by a thread, but otherwise it looked good.

Wendell Swain was sitting on a chair pulled up to Bella's bedside. They were holding hands, or at least Wendell was. Tiny observed them silently from the doorway. They looked as if they had been having words. This was an expression Tiny liked, as if words, like doughnuts, left telltale dust on your lips.

"Am I interrupting something?" he said.

Wendell stood up, quickly. "Uh, no," he said. Then he did a double take, the way you do when a rabbit is standing at the door, holding a dozen helium-filled balloons. "Oh, it's you," he said. He chuckled. It was one of his charms. Wendell was the handsomest boy at H. P. Lovecraft High: school president, captain of everything, scholar, saint, and master of the sociable chuckle. He was not on his game today, however, Tiny noted. It was a hollow kind of chuckle that fizzled out pretty quickly. Wendell looked drained and slightly dazed. "I was just leaving," he said.

"Good," said Tiny, stepping decisively into the room. "Bella and I need to talk." He stared at her. Her dark eyes gathered him in, drew him toward her. It was an uncomfortable sensation, as if she were a black hole and he were a dense little planet that had gotten too close.

Wendell sighed. This was highly uncharacteristic. Sighing had not gotten Wendell where he was today. He turned to kiss Bella good-bye. She inclined a pale cheek toward him, but her eyes stayed fixed on Tiny. As Wendell left the room, he bent to whisper in Tiny's floppy ear. "Thanks," he said. "For what you did."

Tiny watched him walk away down the busy corridor, his head down, his hands shoved deep into the pockets of his chinos. Then Tiny turned to Bella. "Wendell looks a little betrayed," he said.

She closed her eyes and let her head sink slowly into her pillow. She appeared to Tiny as if she had been holding her face together with some effort, the way you might hold the shards of a precious porcelain teacup together so that your mother didn't notice you had broken it. She opened her eyes again and seemed dismayed to see Tiny still there. "Why are you dressed like a rabbit?" she asked.

"Because my cowboy costume was at the cleaners," he said.

Bella didn't smile, didn't even pretend. If anything, the gravity in her eyes grew stronger, pulling him closer. "Is my father behind this?" she said. "Did he pay you to come here and cheer me up?"

Tiny shook his head. "No," he said. "Well, unless you count the family château in France he wants me to have." Bella was clearly beyond amusement. Tiny busied himself tying the balloons to her bedpost.

"I'm not a child," she said, glancing disdainfully at the balloons.

"I know," said Tiny. "But I figured there would be loads of flowers."

There were. They were everywhere. "Welcome to my funeral," she said.

Again she closed her eyes, tightly this time, as if by concentrating she might be able to will him away. She folded her arms across her chest, a pale-faced genie, prone and powerless. When she peeked at last, he was at her side. She relented and downgraded her scowl to a petulant grimace. She unfolded her arms, crossed her hands on her bedclothes, and stared resolutely at her fingernails. They were painted a dusky rose. "I know I should be grateful for what you did," she said. "I'm sure you're a big hero at school."

"Correction," said Tiny. "A very *small* hero. But I hear what you're saying, and I didn't come here looking for gratitude."

She glanced at him and away and back again. Her brow furrowed with alarm and then cleared, and her eyes grew large, but she wasn't seeing him anymore, at least, not in his rabbit suit. There was that expression again, thought Tiny. Where had he seen it before? Was it hope or fear?

"You were wearing a lime green bathing cap," she said.

"That must have come as a shock," he said. She

nodded, and for a whole long moment she did not look away. Then whatever it was that had seemed to interest her about him vanished.

"Why are you here?" she asked.

"I've taken you on," he said. "The psychiatric team is worried about your recovery. They've decided on radical therapy. Me."

Without looking his way, she arched an eyebrow. "Just my luck," she said. "So what does that mean, exactly?"

Tiny pulled up the chair in which Wendell had been seated only moments earlier. "It means, Bella, I'm your new boyfriend." He held up both hands against the protest that blazed in her eyes. "I know, I know," he said quickly. "It is an extreme measure. Frankly, I was surprised when Dr. Gupta approached me. But there seemed no other way. I assure you, I will not take advantage of my position."

This elicited a wry smile. But a wry smile was better than nothing, thought Tiny. It was good to see her lips twist upward. Such full lips, and so deathly pallid.

"I'm glad you won't take advantage," she said. "So we'll just talk?" She laughed, a stunted and cynical little laugh. "Because, it's the talkers that are worst, you know. 'I just want to talk,' they plead. 'Really,' they insist. But all their words have hands in them, and the sentences they compose tend to lean against you whenever they get a chance."

Tiny stood up and freed one of the balloons from the pack, a yellow one.

"Actually," said Bella, "even worse than the talkers are the guys who want to put you on a pedestal. Their eyes honor you with every glance, but you're a freak to them. You might as well be something in a museum with two heads."

With nimble fingers Tiny untied the knot in the balloon and held the bladder to his lips. He sucked in three quick breaths of helium. Gently he touched her arm to make her look at him.

"To be, or not to be, that is the question," he said. He sounded just like a Smurf. She smiled despite herself.

III

When the call came, Tiny was watching a video of *Monty Python,* the "Upper-Class Twit of the Year" sketch. He paused it just as one of the twits raised a gun to his head.

"He didn't look betrayed," said Bella without a word of introduction. "He looked *offended.* He can't understand how anyone who had him for a boyfriend would want to kill herself."

"Isn't 'offended' kind of the same thing as 'betrayed'?" said Tiny.

"No," she said. "I've been thinking about this all day. I insulted him. 'Betrayed' kind of means you were on the same side, had the same goals. You have to be a team before you can be betrayed. That wasn't Wendell and me. *Our* goals were Wendell's goals. *Our* future was Wendell's future."

"Ahhh," said Tiny. "That explains why you tried to kill yourself." He clicked the Off button and watched the twit on the TV screen implode into blackness.

"If we're going to go out together, Tiny, you can't be smug and patronizing," she said. "I hate that. The ones who want to transform you. 'You're so beautiful,' they say. 'All you need is a personality—my personality!' "

"Like Henry Higgins," said Tiny.

"Who?"

"It's not important. What about just being you?"

"Look who's talking," she said.

There was nothing Tiny could say. Nothing Bella could say, either.

There was a long silence on the line. Tiny could hear hospital sounds, the echoing voice of someone paging Dr. Someone. Then Bella spoke again, her voice thin and tired. "I thought being with Wendell would make me a someone," she said. "I was wrong."

Tiny waited a respectful moment. "Being a someone is overrated," he said.

She chuckled—something she'd obviously picked up from Wendell. "I can't believe a rabbit just told me being a someone is overrated."

"I meant now," said Tiny. "Being a someone now and having to be a teenager at the same time—forget it. And, I'll have you know, I'm not dressed as a rabbit tonight."

"No? What are you wearing?"

"What is this, some kind of 900 service?" he said. "Are you billing me by the minute?"

She laughed. It occurred to Tiny that she didn't seem to have much practice. It was a wobbly laugh; training wheels held it upright. But it came from inside her; it wasn't something she had borrowed, and for that Tiny was pleased. Progress, he thought.

"So?" she said at last, her voice all husky and kittenish. "What *are* you wearing, Mr. Rathbone?"

"Something with a lot of chiffon," he said. "Something Grace Kelly might have worn in *Rear Window.*"

She laughed again. "You and your costumes," she said. "What's that about, anyway?"

"It's about pretending," said Tiny. "Like those butterflies that have big evil-looking eyes on their wings to scare off predators."

"Sort of reverse camouflage," she said.

"Exactly."

IV

Tiny picked up Bella in a blue convertible, the kind of blue you only saw in fifties movies. She had been released. She was home now, but not back at school yet, and he was the only person she was allowed to see. Doctor's orders. Her parents smiled at him, their arms entwined. He was dressed like Cary Grant in *To Catch a Thief.* A very small Cary Grant.

"You kids have a good time," said her father.

"I hope you'll stay for dinner, Tiny," said her mother.

Bella was wearing flat sandals, which was thoughtful of her. She was in a breezy summer dress with no sleeves. "You can drive?" she asked as he opened the door for her.

"Sure," he said, and pointed to a pile of books on the driver's seat. "I find art books are the most comfortable. I used a booster seat for a while, but it ruined my image."

It was a beautiful day, late May. The lilacs were in bloom. He drove her to his cottage on Shallow Lake. They talked the whole way. At one point she looked at him with concern on her face. "Your sunglasses," she said. She took them, gently, from his nose. She breathed on each dark lens and then buffed them with the hem of her dress until they were spotless.

She put them lightly back in place, her hand brushing his cheek as she did.

"Thank you, darling. I don't know what I'd do without you," he said. He had Cary Grant down pat.

He was going to teach her how to water-ski. It was part of her therapy. "Trust me," he said. He had brought along a wet suit for her. The air was hot but the lake was still cold. She changed in the cottage while he got the boat ready. By the time she arrived on the dock, there was low thunder over the distant hills.

"It's a long way off," he said. "You'll be all right."

She was nervous. She sat on the lip of the dock, fumbling with the skis. One of them fell into the water and drifted off. Tiny had to wade out to recover it. Summer lightning flashed.

"I don't know about this," she said.

"It's safe," said Tiny. "As long as you're with me."

There should have been a third person with them, someone to mind the skier, but Tiny, selfishly, wanted her all to himself. And besides, it was a week-day; there weren't many people out. He skippered the boat with ease, and, more important, he knew this lake like the back of his hand.

"Keep your arms straight," he coached her. "Your back just a little arched. Not too much. Don't fight the towline."

Lightning flashed. Thunder rolled, closer now, though the sky above the lake was still achingly blue.

"Won't I get electrocuted?" she asked.

"Not if you stay up," he said.

"Why do I have to do this, again?" she said.

Tiny was in the boat now, drifting away from her, letting the towline play out. "Keep your tips up!" he shouted over his shoulder.

It took her seven tries. She wanted to quit after three. By the fifth time she was shuddering terribly, but by then she refused to give up. The sky had darkened. It started to rain, lightly. "We'll start from the water," she said. Her lips were blue. "I don't want to go back to the dock. It's colder out of the water than in it."

She almost got it that time. And then, on her seventh attempt, she did. He thought she was going

222

to fall, but she righted herself, found her balance, leaned back. Relaxed.

They went for miles. Out of the bay, out onto the wide, wide lake. Then the rain picked up and the lightning drew nearer and Tiny circled back toward the cottage. He had forgotten to explain to her about how to land, but she figured it out, landing brilliantly, letting go of the towline, instinctively, at the exact right moment, and gliding into the dock.

By the time he had moored the boat and thrown a tarp over it, she had changed into some old cottage clothes and found the makings for hot chocolate. Tiny built a roaring fire in the fireplace and changed. The storm crashed around outside, angry about something, bending the trees and bushes as if looking for someone.

"I was good, wasn't I," she said. It wasn't a question.

"You were great," he said.

"I mean, it took so long, but when I got it, I got it. Right?"

"Right."

Thunder crashed directly overhead. The cottage

223

shook. Rain lashed the window. Bella cuddled close to him. Then she pulled away, all of a sudden, so that she could look him square in the face. Her color was back. Her skin was like moonlight on a sandy beach. Her eyes were like bright brown pebbles in a stream. Her hair caught some of the fire and some of the storm and looked like tarnished gold coins. Suddenly he knew where he had seen her before.

"You wanted me to know I could do it," she said. "Stand up on my own two feet. That was the therapy, right?"

He nodded. "It's called Shallow Lake," he said. "But I call it High Lake." He was talking too loudly. He didn't know why. "Because it's like high school," he said. He turned away from the fire and pointed over the back of the couch, through the picture window. "Over there, across the lake, that's Graduation Beach."

She nodded. "I get it," she said, smiling. "It's a metaphor."

"Correction," he said. "It's a lake. There are shoals and deadheads and other boaters and lone, long-distance swimmers."

"You don't need to yell," she said, although she did not seem really perturbed.

"You have to keep your tips up," said Tiny.

"I get it, I get it," she said, laughing aloud, a stable laugh, an unswerving laugh, a laugh that did not need supports of any kind.

V

Tiny changed his end-of-the-year skit. It started in front of closed curtains. He stood on the edge of the stage, wearing a dark suit, a white shirt, and a crisp blue tie. He carried a briefcase and, from time to time, looked anxiously to stage left and checked his watch, a commuter waiting for his train. But the train never came. Skis came, instead, down from the flies, like manna from heaven, accompanied by the *boom, boom, boom, boom* Strauss theme from *2001: A Space Odyssey*. In the briefcase, he discovered a lime green bathing cap and an orange flotation device, which he put on over the suit. Then he took his place on the lip of the stage, with his feet dangling over the edge, dead center, under a hot

225

special, alone, or so it seemed. Loud music came up—live music!—and with it the curtains rose, and there were all five of the thrash bands, and they were all dressed in suits and flotation devices. Then Maury joined in on the trombone, Tiffany and Melissa danced, and all the comics and folkies and jocks crowded onto the stage to sing along. Tiny had written a song that Rupert Blitzstein set to music. It was about not sinking. It had a simple chorus—"On the high school lake, keep your tips up"—and everyone at H. P. Lovecraft High joined in.

Bella came to see him backstage. Everyone was gone by then. She lifted him up and placed him on a riser and hugged him and told him he was brilliant. That's when he showed her the book. They sat together on the edge of the empty stage in the empty house.

"I feel so stupid," he said. "I knew your face reminded me of someone, and I was sitting on it the whole time."

It was one of the art books Tiny kept on the driver's seat to make him tall enough to see where he was going. It was a book about Michelangelo's paintings in the Sistine Chapel.

"Here," he said. And there she was. Bella. It was a detail, a close-up. There was a crack in the paint across her right eyelid and trailing across her forehead to her hairline.

"It is me," she said, in wonder. "But who am I?" So he flipped back a page and she gasped. "I know this painting," she said.

"Everyone knows this painting," said Tiny.

It was *The Creation of Adam,* where God reaches out his incredibly muscular right arm and Adam reaches out his incredibly muscular left arm and their fingers almost touch. And across the space between their fingers, the spark of life is about to jump, the way a thought jumps the space between neurons. Adam reclined on a little green chunk of Eden. God hung suspended in a pink cloth cloud, surrounded by angels. But under his left arm, close to his heart, was the woman with the beautiful face. She was staring down at Adam, her eyes full of fascination and trepidation.

Bella laughed, shocked. "I've seen this painting a hundred times and I never saw her."

"That's because Michelangelo is such a genius," said Tiny, a little sadly. "All anyone ever sees is those two fingers. It's what Michelangelo *wants* us to see. It kind of blinds a person. All you can see after that is Adam, because he's so big and so incredibly nude, and God, because he's so . . . well, Godlike."

By now, Bella had taken the book onto her own lap and was staring at the picture, staring, Tiny could tell, at her likeness. "But who am I supposed to be?" she asked, so quietly he barely heard her.

"Eve," said Tiny. "Just before she was created but as she already existed in the mind of God."

"Oh," said Bella. She stared a bit longer before she could remove her eyes from the image on the page. Then, reluctantly, Tiny took the book away from her. Because it was time. "Well, there you go," she said.

Tiny closed the book. And held it tightly in his arms. He closed his eyes and rocked back and forth, back and forth. He could feel her beside him pondering the picture in her heart. So close. So close.

"Tiny?"

It was Horace, the custodian. He was standing right where Mr. Hurd stood when he was conducting the school band. Tiny hadn't heard him coming. "You OK?" said Horace.

Tiny shook his head. Horace hoisted himself up onto the stage beside him. He didn't say anything.

"She was calling out," said Tiny. "She heard me thumping around up here, working on my skit, and she was calling out for help."

Horace patted him gently on the knee. "You can't blame yourself," he said. "That poor girl had her mind made up."

"No," said Tiny. "That's the problem. Her mind wasn't made up at all."

Crazy, Beautiful

Jacqueline Woodson

I will give you this—a few moments in my life. Do with them as you wish. They are yours now. I was twelve then and even as I write this, twelve is leaving, going away from me. Tomorrow, I will be sixteen, and maybe sixteen is twelve all over again—a different body, a fuzzier brain, boys draping into vision everywhere, girls mysterious now—new to me and old, too. I will tell you all I remember. Then I will be free of twelve—allowed to move on. Where I will go from here—even though the years have passed, I do not know. For at this moment, I am twelve still—tall, lanky, unsure. My hair has been straightened, parted in the center, and pulled into two braids. At the end of each braid is an elastic—pink, perhaps, or sky blue. These are my favorite colors and I wear them often. It is summery today—bright morning and I am wearing sky blue shorts and a sky blue top. In cursive iron-on letters, my name moves across my flat chest—*Angela*—scripted like a promise of something I do not yet understand. Somewhere far off someone is calling my name now. I have a small gap between my two front teeth. Otherwise my teeth are straight and white and my smile is the only part of me that feels pretty. I am not pretty. The pretty girls surround me, move past without seeing anyone but others like them. Their skin is clear. Their bodies are beginning to curve into something—something that will make them even prettier. Their laughter makes others smile. Their fingers are long. Some are short-haired and some aren't, but the way the hair moves around the face takes the breath—and holds it. The pretty girls don't see me. How can they? I am not beautiful. I am not here. Then, where am I?

I am the tallest girl in my class, and when my classmates want to be mean, they yell, *Here comes the Jolly Green Giant.* The taunt echoes through schoolyards and hallways. *Comes . . . comes . . . comes. Giant . . . giant . . . giant.*

But it is summer now and I do not have to line up in size order anywhere. I do not have to listen to the taunting of classmates. No, it is summer. July perhaps. Or early August. Hot already. I am standing with my hands on my hips. Waiting. Behind me, someone keeps calling my name, but I ignore this. My block is clean this morning. This first clear day after a week of rain, my grandmother and other mothers came out to sweep damp newspaper, potato chip and candy wrappers, and brown paper bags into the street. This morning, the street-cleaning truck cruised by—bleach-scented water and heavy black brushes taking our trash, and everyone else's, with it. It was early but already hot, and I stood there, my shorts pulled up, my feet bare—letting the truck's cool, smelly water breeze over me. My head back, my dark arms out like wings, my T-shirt growing damp.

The sweepers had all gone inside by then, my grandmother complaining, *Looks like nobody lives here* even as my front yard brightened with the absence of trash, even as a small breeze pushed the pale curtains lovingly through my family's windows. In the mist of the street cleaner, I was alone. And even as the water cooled me, a sadness crept up, out of my very bones, pushing through marrow and blood and skin to drape me in itself. It was not unfamiliar, this sadness. But as always, it surprised me, seeming to come at once from no place and from the deepest parts of me.

233

C'mon, Angie, I been calling you for like a year already.

And now I turn in the hot afternoon to find my best friend standing beside me. Where I am dark, she is olive. Where my hair is straightened, hers curls down her back, ringlets circling her face. Where I am still flat chested and skinny, she is not. She is beautiful, and although we have been friends since we were five years old, I worry that the day will come when she will realize I am not beautiful like she is, that this will suddenly matter to her, and the seven years of friendship will mean nothing. But today is not the day. Today she stands before me dressed in pale pink shorts and a T-shirt with *Maria* across the front. Although we often dress alike, Maria's mother is more daring than my own, allowing Maria to wear the clothes of the moment—miniskirts and go-go boots, ankle-length leather coats and platform shoes. I am confined to flat shoes and practical cottons—clothes my mother swears will feel better and last longer.

Get your sister for double Dutch, Maria says, holding up the long cord we talked the telephone man into giving us.

She won't want to. Think of somebody else.

This is the year my sister is moving away from us. She is fourteen, and there is a far-off look in her eyes. Her brilliance has been discovered—by teachers and social workers and everyone on the block. But while this is a moment I dream of often—to wake up understanding math and science and geography—my sister has moved inside herself, to a quiet place I do not understand. She sits for hours now, a bowl of popcorn and a glass of water next to her on the end table, with books whose words are as foreign to me as the understanding of pi and Fe and the USSR open on her lap. She reads with no sense of who is around her, what is happening in the room, on the block, in the world. When she closes a book at the end of the day, she looks up, surprised, it seems, that there is a world and she is in it still. We call her Einstein and Freak Show and any other name that will get her to react—to *see us.* Us regular, not-brilliant kids who are stuck right here on earth.

There is a stillness to the air. Down the block, three boys are playing Skully—shooting tar-filled bottle tops over a diagram of numbers drawn with chalk on the street. They crouch down on their knees, their butts up in the air, and use their thumbs and pointers to shoot the tops. I am not allowed to play this game. Not allowed to crouch down like this. My mother doesn't allow it and my friends don't. *You're not a guy,* Maria says when I speak of my longing to play. Down on the street, their bodies curved into the strange position of the game, the boys look powerful and free and oddly beautiful to me. They crawl around on the warm tar and laugh loudly when one bottle cap knocks another out of the game. Their knees and elbows are dirty. I watch, standing back, away from them. There is something in this game, in their laughter, in the ferocity of their togetherness, that I don't yet understand. When Maria comes close, they duck their heads, look away while looking at her. She smiles at them, then turns quickly away.

C'mon, Angie, Maria says. *You ain't no guy.*

It's not about being no guy, I say. And we sit on the curb and watch them. Her not understanding why I would want to get down in the street, me not knowing how to talk about the word that comes to me: *freedom.* Not knowing now what I will one day know—that Maria already lives the word. That the word, *freedom,* exists for her in the slow turn of her heel, the flip of her dark, curling hair, her thick eyelashes, her smile.

I watch the boys while Maria untangles the rope. How many games of double Dutch have we played this summer? How many games of hopscotch and Miss Lucy and handball? How many times have we run across the street to the park, climbed onto the swings, and tried to touch tree leaves with our toes?

This summer there is a longing in me so deep, I feel some mornings that I will drown in it. A longing to *be*long. Not to my friends or my block, but to *me* somehow. To grow into my skin and hair and gap-teeth. To know what I feel, like everyone around me already knows or doesn't care to know. Who am I?

When the boys look past me, who am I?

When the kids call me Jolly Green Giant, who am I?

When the grown-ups talk about my manners and my long legs that I'll *grow into,* who am I?

When I lean into the bathroom mirror, trying to find the beauty there, who . . . ?

237

It is Thursday night and my grandmother is brushing my hair. She pulls the brush quickly through it. Then there are the hard plastic teeth of the comb making a part down the center of my scalp. The kitchen is quiet. On the stove what is left of this evening's meal remains—okra that I hate, fried chicken that I love, and mashed potatoes that I can either take or leave. Tonight, because my grandmother has used skim milk in them instead of whole, I have left them. Now my grandmother pulls the left side of my hair into a tight braid as she lectures me.

That's why you so skinny now, she says. *Clothes just hanging off of you. I shouldn't even have told you I used skim milk. You wouldn't have known the difference.*

Yes, I would've. They tasted different.

Different how?

Nasty different. Like potato water.

My grandmother taps the comb against my head. It is a firm tap but not a mean one.

Shouldn't even have told you. You would've eaten them right up.

She braids my hair to the very end, and the neat, tight braids stop at my shoulder before curling up. This year I want to be able to comb my own hair, but when my grandmother holds out the brush and comb with a stubborn *Go on, then. Comb your nappy hair,* I don't. Her hands are too sure, too strong. Too familiar.

My sister pulls her own hair back into a ponytail. I am told I have my father's hair—thick, crinkled, jet-black. My sister's curls are looser, falling over her face and down her back in a way that my grandmother says her own mother's hair once fell. I do not understand how my sister and I got such different hair.

As my grandmother puts an elastic on the second braid, I say, *I wanted a ponytail like Dana's.*

My grandmother looks at me as though I've lost my mind. *Then you better grow some hair like Dana's.*

Outside, it is nearly dark. I stand by the window and wait for my brothers and sister to finish dressing. *You better grow some hair like Dana's.* I know there is love and laughter and my grandmother's own strange sense of humor in this statement. Still, it hurts. As I stand, dressed in a white cotton blouse and sky blue wraparound skirt, I can see my sister behind me—her reflection in the windowpane clear and sure. She is tall like I am. When her breasts grew, she was no longer skinny but thin. One day, maybe I will have breasts and be thin. When we dress alike, people often ask if we are twins—same dark skin and gap-teeth. Same nose—long but broad. Dark eyes, thick brows and lashes. Our cheekbones jut up out of our faces in a way that makes strangers comment. *Look at those bones,* they say. *Such strong bones,* they say. *Fraternal twins,* they say. *Different hair, though.*

Of course not, my sister says. *I'm older. Can't you tell? Jeez.*

But there is something else to my sister. Something that makes her the beautiful one. I don't know what this something is, but I see it in the eyes of relatives and strangers. The way their looks linger. The way fear marches across their faces and dissolves their own confidence.

Why are you just standing staring out at the darkness? my sister wants to know now.

I shrug. *No reason. Just thought I saw something.*

Every Monday, Thursday, Saturday, and Sunday, there is religion. This Thursday evening is no exception. We have always been Jehovah's Witnesses, the way my friends are born Catholics and Protestants and Seventh Day Adventists. Our religion is as much a part of us as the color of our skin. We know who God is and why. We believe in Christ and everlasting life. We don't curse and we're not supposed to lie or steal. We carry briefcases with the literature of our religion. As my grandmother locks the door behind us, we wait at our front gate—my brothers, my sister, and I dressed like little adults. My younger brother is nine years old. He pulls uncomfortably at his tie and shrugs out of his sport coat in the summer heat.

I'll put it on when we get there, he says when my grandmother starts to speak. He is my grandmother's favorite, and we all know this so none of us questions it, and nobody else attempts to remove an article of clothing.

I am a Jehovah's Witness. I say this at the beginning of each school year, and upon hearing it, my teachers understand—this one is the one who will leave when we stand to recite the Pledge of Allegiance. This one will not participate in any holiday celebrations. No Secret Santa for this one. No Valentine. No birthday cupcake on this one's desk. No candle's bright promise of something better to come. I am a Jehovah's Witness and have been so all of my life. My Bible is highlighted and dog-eared. I believe this world will end with fire and brimstone and this ending is soon to come. I believe there are two roads—a wide one and a narrow one. Upon the wide road, people dance and curse and celebrate holidays. The narrow road is less crowded, and those walking it walk with their heads turned toward God. There will come a time, my grandmother promises, when the walkers of the narrow road will have cause to celebrate.

This system of things will be destroyed, and we'll live in a new world, a beautiful paradise on earth.

My mother will not be a part of this paradise. As we walk away from our building, I turn to look where the curtains billow from the upstairs windows. My mother is in there somewhere. Maybe she is lying on her side, reading one of the many romance novels she owns. In the novels, white women with flowing hair live in wealthy communities with servants and beautiful clothes. They meet handsome men who love them deeply and endlessly. My mother turns the pages slowly, hoping to linger in this place. My mother is not a Jehovah's Witness. Although she believes in God, she does not go with us when we leave for the Kingdom Hall. In our few hours away from her, she lets herself get lost in worlds she'll never know. Her new world. Her paradise on earth.

In her world now Al Green is singing, *Lay your head upon my pillow* . . . and maybe she is moving gently around the living room now, swaying to Al's deep voice. Maybe she has the broom in her hands, imagining the broom is the man who will rescue her from this system of things, this world that still confuses her. Maybe she is asking, *How did I get four children? And me only thirty-four.*

I walk slowly down our block—trailing behind my grandmother, brothers, and sister. Behind me I can hear kids taunting, *Churchie, churchie, churchie. Churchie, churchie, churchie.* Too many times, my sister has turned to them and shouted, *It's not church, it's a Kingdom Hall, you morons.* But tonight she doesn't. We walk with our backs straight, our eyes directly in front of us. We walk down the block and away from it. The sun has set. The road is narrow. Our heads are turned slightly upward. Toward God.

Lourdes and Gabriella are twins. Not identical. But when they put on their Catholic school uniforms, it is harder to tell them apart. They are pale skinned and gray eyed, their white-blond hair making us think of albinos. We whisper this—*How can their mothers love them, and them so ugly like that?* They have two brothers. One brother is seven and normal. The other is four and not. This is the one we tease. His name is Ramon, and he sits in his window with the elbow of his left arm in the palm of his right hand. For hours, he shakes the left arm and stares at it. Lourdes and her family move onto our block in May. Before long, we are all imitating her brother. When we see Lourdes we do as her brother does. We say, *Hey, pale girl, watch this.* And pretend that this is the way one says hello. Lourdes and Gabriella are twelve. The day after they move in, they sit on the stoop with their brothers and watch the rest of us. Cautiously. Looking away when we look back— except Ramon, who stares full on at us, shaking his arm. When I look at him full on, he smiles, a smile for all of us—aimless and open.

You know how to jump? Maria asks, holding out the rope. And Lourdes and her sister shake their heads.

Where'd you move from that you don't know how to jump? And Lourdes and her sister shrug.

You don't know where you moved from? I ask.

They shrug again. Gabriella says, *For us to know, for you to find out.*

Like anybody really cares, Maria says. *Must be Mars if you can't jump.*

Some other kids have come closer to listen and now *Oooooh's* ripple through the crowd. These are fighting words. I turn and stare nervously up at my window. My mother is in there somewhere. My grandmother, too. If I am standing anywhere near a fight, I'll be in trouble. Our house is full of rules. I am learning that the two most ridiculous ones are *don't fight* and *don't come home with your butt beat, either.* I put my hands in my pockets and move a little bit away from everything. Because this move isn't new for me, I've been labeled a chicken, a chump, and a bunch of other names I'd get in a lot of trouble if I said. Somewhere far off, an ambulance siren is going, moving closer. We all look toward the sound, watch the ambulance speed down the avenue that is at one end of our block. The sun, high up and hot, moves behind a cloud. As the siren fades, Maria says, *You act like you wanna jump in my face.*

We look at Gabriella, and I say a silent prayer: *Please jump in her face, but please everybody move around the corner so my mother doesn't see me watching a fight.*

Like I want to get anywhere near your ugly face, Gabriella says. And for a moment no one speaks, our confusion thick and silent as the heat. How can she not know, we wonder, that Maria and, by extension, all of us are the beautiful ones? How can Gabriella, with her pale skin and watery eyes, not see Maria's beauty? How can she flip her own near-white hair and not tear up at the weight and life in Maria's dark curls. We don't know how to ask this—this simple and crazy question—*How could you possibly not know?*

And we don't know how to ask it. None of us. Maria throws the moves fast toward her. I take another step back, my stomach rising up with both excitement and fear. Then everyone is screaming and my mother is at the window, threatening every kid in the group, name by name. But Maria and Gabriella don't hear her, and in another minute my mother is hurrying across the street, stepping between them. Maria's face is unmarked, but Gabriella's is now covered with scratches, thick red lines moving every which way. Maybe she is crying. Maybe, later on, she will look into her mirror and understand then what we already know.

Hours later, sitting on my own stoop, I stare out at our block. Some boys are still playing Skully, but the clouds have moved in. After a few minutes, a steady summer rain begins to fall. I stick my tongue out, taste the drops—hear, still, the echo of my mother's threats. There will be no going to Maria's house to play now— not for at least a week. And for at least a week I will have to hear about what a bad influence Maria is, how wild. *Where is her mother, anyway?* my own mother will say over and over. *And don't go across the street near those new girls, either. Can't believe people let their kids act the fool.* On and on and on. The rain is cool on my tongue. If water was a color, it would be sky blue. That's the taste of it. Soft. Light. Free.

I hold out my hand. Stare down at my long, dark arm. *Whose beauty is this?* I will ask one day. *Whose beauty is this?*

Across the street, Lourdes and Gabriella glare out over the nearly empty block, their faces twisting between sadness and confusion. But Ramon gives everyone and no one his crazy, beautiful smile. Holds his elbow in his hand and, for a moment, looks as though he's asking us all . . . to come closer.

Reader's Guide

Book Summary

Such a Pretty Face, despite its title, isn't going to make you prettier, at least not in the physical sense. It may make you *feel* more beautiful, though. The stories collected here talk about the subtle, infinite variations of beauty and the possibility of finding it, within yourself or close at hand.

In exploring beauty, the authors acknowledge our culture's obsession with physical perfection, often as defined by the media, but they refuse to accept beauty's myths. Their stories redefine beauty, showing that it can be a stunning moment of self-recognition, or a friend who knows when to sit without judgment at your side, or a moment in nature, or one special person who charms you with his or her honesty or uniqueness. Real beauty is more than a pretty face.

Discussion Questions

1) What are the unwritten rules for the physically beautiful, depicted in Ron Koertge's short story,

"Such a Pretty Face"? Are Melissa's efforts to negotiate these rules successful? Do you observe unwritten rules or expectations for those who are deemed beautiful in your own world or group of friends?

2) "I felt sorry. For her. 'Cause you know what? I really liked her. And you know what? In those moments when I could stop seeing me where she was supposed to be? Cherry was really pretty," says the narrator in Chris Lynch's "Red Rover, Red Rover." Why can't he see Cherry's beauty when he sees himself in her?

3) What does it mean to be swan beautiful in a family full of ducks, or duck beautiful in a family full of swans, in Jamie Pittel's story, "What I Look Like"? In what ways do you believe most teens feel swan beautiful in a world of ducks?

4) Mary Ann Rodman's story, "Farang," looks at cultural beauty. In this story, the Thai girls try to be more American, and the American girls lust to be thin and tiny like the Thai girls. The protagonist,

Lauren, recognizes that there's a different sort of beauty inside each person's heart. "But good hearts don't show," she concludes, "the way that light skin and long shiny hair do." What does she mean when she draws this conclusion? Do you agree or disagree that this is the way it is?

5) In the story "Ape," protagonist Ford Gordon talks about the myth of uniformity and conformity, explaining that his grandfather, who immigrated to the United States at a time when Greeks were looked on suspiciously, hid his heritage by changing his name to Gordon. Ford himself has learned to blend in by ridding himself of a Boston accent. He says, "Now I speak a perfect California tongue, flavorless as tap water. Here in Sacramento, people converse with perfectly blended uniformity, as similar as the pastel tract homes we live in." Still, he stands out because of his physical appearance. When he tries to hide his hirsute appearance in order to blend in, Ford is giving in to contemporary myths about physical beauty. He is taking

them on as reality. What are some beauty myths, and how do we act when we believe they are our reality?

6) "I think it's payback because I *like* being beautiful. Because . . . maybe I'm not so nice to people who aren't," says Zelly of her truly bad-hair-day experience in Lauren Myracle's short story, "Bad Hair Day." Zelly and her best friend, Kristin, agree that everyone makes secret fun of others' flaws. Even their saintly friend, Scout, probably says mean things behind people's backs. Do you think this is true, that most or all people poke fun at others when their flaws become apparent?

7) Beauty, in Norma Fox Mazer's story, "How to Survive a Name," recognizes early on that she is no beauty, but it is a note from a classmate that makes her realize how much it hurts to know others see this lack of beauty. How does she handle this realization?

8) After Tiny finds the semiconscious Bella under the stage trapdoor in Tim Wynne-Jones's story, "Bella

in Five Acts," he tries to help her find beauty in life. For Tiny, what is beauty? How does he bring this beauty to his world?

9) Tiny tells Bella that in crossing over High Lake to Graduation Beach, you need to keep your tips up. What does he mean with this metaphor? How is he keeping his own metaphoric tips up?

10) Ellen Wittlinger's "Cheekbones" allows readers to see more than one response to physical beauty through the eyes of Lucy and her mother. How do the two characters view the importance of physical beauty? Is there one correct interpretation?

11) The loss of physical beauty plays a small role in Anita Riggio's "Bingo," but this is actually a story about Peter Roscoe learning to appreciate the natural beauty of life through his friendship with Maeve. What does it take for Peter to recognize all that he has?

12) In Jacqueline Woodson's story, "My Crazy, Beautiful World," readers watch Angela face the

shock of seeing herself and her group through the eyes of outsiders. In seeing herself this way, how does Angela define beauty in her own life?

13) Two stories, Louise Hawes's "Sideshow" and J. James Keels's "Ape," contain references to carnival freak shows, where carnival-goers would pay to look at people who stood out from the norm, people considered freaks. Why do you think that the theme of beauty would draw writers to consider these shows?

Writing Activities

1) Tiny, in "Bella in Five Acts," tells Bella that Shallow Lake, the lake where his family owns a cottage, is in his mind High Lake. He says some people water- ski and others swim across to Graduation Beach. He has learned that, if you plan to ski across, you have to keep your tips up. Write about the method you would use to cross the lake and include what you've learned about the possible problems or obstacles in making this crossing.

2) Write about a time when you learned something about how you experience beauty in your world.

CREATIVE ART

1) Using magazine cutouts, drawings, words, and phrases, create a collage that defines beauty as you perceive it.

2) Create a collection of found objects that depict natural beauty. List words to describe beauty and create a list poem that can be placed with your collection.

3) Using whatever media you wish, draw or paint your vision of beauty.

AN INTERVIEW WITH THE EDITOR

Q: What attracted you to creating an anthology about beauty?

A: It seems that all my life I've watched how definitions of beauty affect the people around me. Growing up, I never felt I could measure up to physical standards of beauty. I was short, my nose was soooo long, my hair was as straight and frizzy as Janis Joplin's—and I didn't even have her voice.

Over the next decade, models grew thinner and thinner. By then I was teaching, and I saw my female students attempt to emulate them. All these beautiful people, with curving bodies and wide smiles, seemed to grow gaunt and pinched.

Then when I had my own culturally mixed family, I saw how my children went through stages in which they compared themselves to their siblings. Their differences became perceived flaws, and they felt they came up short. Our culture had created an obsession with looks and with an ideal that is impossible. It seemed that, everywhere I looked, we were all in danger of losing our sense of ourselves as beautiful to something that wasn't ideal at all.

Meanwhile, the world is full of such natural beauty—everything from thunderstorms that light up the sky to reveal startling sights, or gentle winds that push leaves in swirls against stone buildings, to good people with generous hearts and souls.

But sometimes, we get lost in our obsession with the airbrushed pages of celebrity and model "beauty." We lose the ability to see the truly gorgeous aspects of life around us.

I wanted to gather writers who had demonstrated their own beauty through their written work, but also through friendship and through mentoring one another, to create an anthology that challenged cultural expectations and redefined beauty in broader terms, on their individual terms.

Q: When selecting the stories for this anthology, what did you look for?

A: I looked for stories that offered fresh perspectives through an individual character's experience. I wanted each story to give the reader pause, a chance to reconsider what is, in fact, beautiful. I wasn't looking for only stories about the physically beautiful; I wanted to see beauty in each story from an emotionally or even spiritually aesthetic perspective.

Q: Your very first story is about a physically beautiful girl, so beautiful that no one can relate to her. Why did you include that story? Isn't it just encouraging stereotypes of beauty?

A: In order to live up to a physical ideal, those who support that ideal create expectations that become unwritten rules. The "beautiful" people in our world are given a tremendous amount of privilege and attention, but it sometimes costs them the freedom to be who they really are. Some of this occurs because the rules for beauty are that you must always be beautiful; nothing less is allowed, and nothing more is expected. You shouldn't get your hands dirty, and you don't need a brain. Don't ever allow yourself to be ugly. Attention and admiration aren't earned, because all that the beautiful person must do is be physically attractive. The beautiful person is shunned if he or she deviates from these expectations, and so that person is often made to feel shallow, undeserving, and isolated. Ridiculous ideals of physical beauty hurt everyone—even those who come closest to meeting them.

257

Q: You include stories in which characters behave badly toward others, particularly the older brother in "Sideshow." How does behavior define beauty?

A: The stories that captured ugliness in its rawest form were those that captured truly hurtful behavior, which is truly ugly. To define true beauty, I thought it was important to recognize what is ugly. By arranging these stories next to stories that capture natural beauty or beautiful moments or behavior, true beauty is heightened because we can see the extremes.

About the Contributors

Louise Hawes, who lives outside Chapel Hill, North Carolina, has written books for all ages, her last three for young adults. *Rosey in the Present Tense* was an ALA Popular Paperback of 2000; *Waiting for Christopher* was a 2003 New York Public Library Best Book for the Teen Age; and *The Vanishing Point,* a 2005 New York Public Library Best Book for the Teen Age, was also nominated as an ALA Best Book for Young Adults. Louise, whose first picture book debuted in 2006, will prove she "covers the waterfront" when the University Press of Mississippi publishes a collection of her short fiction for adults in 2007. "Beauty," she claims, "is not an inherent quality, but a perception, a moment. Everyone and everything is beautiful sometime, and no one and nothing can be beautiful forever." For more on Louise, check out www.louisehawes.com.

J. James Keels has self-published chapbooks, contributed to various underground zines, and read at Bay Area poetry readings. He holds a BA in sociology and human sexuality studies from San

Francisco State University. He later received an MFA in writing from Vermont College. A regular faculty member of the Community College of Vermont, he is now an MA candidate in elementary education at Johnson State College. He lives in Vermont and is currently at work on a young adult novel. "Physical beauty," he says, "has nothing to do with those unrealistic, unhealthy media images many strive toward. Beauty comes with self-actualization—from our own unique substance. Beauty cannot be planned or calculated. Beauty cannot be purchased in a store. When we are true to ourselves, and not external pressures, we are truly fabulous."

Ron Koertge is a master at capturing teenagers' voices—often in witty repartee—and that is fully evident in his *Margaux with an X*, the story of a sharp-tongued beauty and a quirky, quick-witted loner. Another unlikely pairing is found in *Stoner & Spaz*, Ron's funny, in-your-face tale of a young cinephile with cerebral palsy and the stoner who steals his heart. A faculty member for more than thirty-five years at Pasadena City College, he taught everything from Shakespeare to remedial writing. In addition to his young adult novels, Ron writes poetry. His novel in poetry *Shakespeare Bats Cleanup* is entirely in free verse, with examples of several poetic forms slipped into the mix, including a sonnet, a haiku, a pastoral, and even a pantoum. *The Brimstone Journals* is another poetry novel, with fifteen different teenage characters narrating four or five poems each. Ron grew up in an agricultural area in an old mining town in Illinois, just across the Mississippi from St. Louis, Missouri. He and his wife live in South Pasadena, California, where, he says, "I like to bet on thoroughbreds, and there's no lovelier sight than having them turn for home with my choice running easy at about ten to one."

Chris Lynch proved he isn't afraid to talk about the difficult emotions in our lives, such as rage, with his novel *Inexcusable,* a 2005 National Book Award finalist. He is the Michael L. Printz Honor Award–winning author of *Freewill* and several other highly acclaimed young adult novels, including *Gold Dust, Iceman, Gypsy Davy,* and *Shadowboxer*—all ALA

Best Books for Young Adults. He is also the author of *Extreme Elvin, Whitechurch,* and *All the Old Haunts.* He holds an MA from the writing program at Emerson College. He mentors aspiring writers and continues to work on new literary projects. He lives in Boston and in Scotland. "My take on beauty?" he says. "Same as everybody else—your beautiful soul, love."

Norma Fox Mazer lives in Montpelier, Vermont, with her husband, the writer Harry Mazer. She has published nearly thirty novels and short-story collections for young adults. Her novels, including *Missing Pieces, Out of Control, When She Was Good,* and the Newbery Honor Book *After the Rain,* are critically acclaimed and popular among young readers for their realistic portrayal of teens in difficult situations. In her novel *Girlhearts,* she brings back the memorable characters from her beloved book *Silver,* who continue to deal with life's hardest moments through their honest and touching relationships. In her new book, *What I Believe,* she tells the story of Vicki through a variety of narrative and poetic forms, including letters, dialogues, free verse, sestinas, pantoums, and even a villanelle. Her character Beauty, in "How to Survive a Name," will be featured in an upcoming novel. She says of beauty, "The word *beautiful* is an abstraction, but useful as shorthand for the almost unbearable pleasure of certain simple, lovely things in this complex world of ours, like the sun setting in a flush of pale green, or a baby gazing fresh at the world."

Lauren Myracle has written many novels for teens and young readers: *Kissing Kate, Eleven, ttyl, Rhymes with Witches, ttfn, The Fashion Disaster That Changed My Life, Twelve,* and *l8r, g8r.* They're all pretty good, and she thinks you should read them. Or not—whatever you please. As far as beauty goes, she has this to say: "People will tell you it's what's on the inside that counts, and they're right. But let's face it, the way we look on the outside plays a big role in the world too. Maybe it shouldn't, but it does. So don't beat yourself up for caring how you look. Just keep some perspective. And if it comes down to painting your nails or saving the world from evil incarnate, well, you know what to do." Visit Lauren at www.laurenmyracle.com.

Jamie Pittel holds an MFA in Writing for Children and Young Adults from Vermont College. Her story "What I Look Like" is excerpted and adapted from a novel in progress titled *The East Pole*. Another story, "Peloria," appeared in *Cicada* magazine. Jamie lives in Somerville, Massachusetts. About beauty, she says, "I think words on a page are beautiful, and chopped vegetables sautéing in a cast-iron pan, and also the ocean. What we look like has a lot to do with how we decorate ourselves."

Anita Riggio has illustrated more than two dozen picture books, six of which she also wrote. "Bingo" is her first published story for young adults. Her first novel, *Jitterbug*, is forthcoming. Anita currently mentors other writers in the low-residency MFA in Creative Writing program at Lesley University in Cambridge, Massachusetts. She and her husband live on a cove in

Connecticut, where they raised their two grown children. Simply put, she says, "Beauty is grace manifested." Learn more about Anita at www.anitariggio.com.

Mary Ann Rodman's books include *Jimmy's Stars* and *Yankee Girl,* both middle-grade novels. She has also written two picture books, *My Best Friend* and *First Grade Stinks.* Music is important to Mary Ann because she always writes to it. She lives in Alpharetta, Georgia, with her husband and daughter. When talking about beauty, Mary Ann defines it personally: "For me, it is a perfectly expressed thought . . . the kind that needs no further clarification or distillation." To find out more about Mary Ann, visit www.maryannrodman.com.

Ellen Wittlinger has published ten novels for young adults and many short stories. One of her books, *Hard Love,* won a Lambda Literary Award and was a Michael L. Printz Honor Book. Her latest novel is *Blind Faith* from Simon & Schuster. She lives in western Massachusetts. "Beauty is that which inspires me," she says. "Most young people are beautiful because of the hope and love and vulnerability that radiate from them. The fact that very few of them believe in their beauty can be heartbreaking." Visit Ellen at www.ellenwittlinger.com.

Jacqueline Woodson recalls the way her fifth-grade teacher's eyes lit up when she said of Jackie's writing, "This is really good." Jackie says that was when "I— the skinny girl in the back of the classroom who was always getting into trouble for talking or missed home-work assignments—sat up a little straighter, folded my hands on the desk, smiled, and began to believe in me." Her books have won numerous awards, includ-ing the YALSA Top Ten Best Books and 2005 YALSA Quick Picks for Reluctant Young Adult Readers for her most recent young adult novel, *Behind You.* Her novel *Show Way* was a 2006 Newbery Honor Book. Her novel in poetry, *Locomotion,* was a National Book Award finalist, a Coretta Scott King Honor Book, and received the 2003 *Boston Globe–Horn Book* Award for fiction. Some other award-winning novels include *Hush, If You Come Softly,* and *Miracle's Boys.* Speaking of beauty, Jackie says, "I think true beauty is having the ability to see 'beauty' in everything—even something 'tragic' or 'heartbreaking.' To not close one's eyes to the world around us, but to be in each moment fully—no matter what." To learn more about Jackie, visit www.jacquelinewoodson.com.

Tim Wynne-Jones says, "Beauty takes your breath away and keeps it in a glass locket. There is no picture in the locket, only your breath, hanging there below her smile." Tim has written more than two dozen books, including adult novels, picture books, short-story anthologies, and young adult novels. He has twice won the Canadian Governor General's Award for children's literature: for *Some of the Kinder Planets* and *The Maestro*. He also won the *Boston Globe–Horn Book* Award for *Planets*. His work has been translated into Japanese, Korean, Danish, Dutch, German, French, Italian, and Catalan. His novel *The Boy in the Burning House* won the Edgar Award from the Mystery Writers of America, and the Arthur Ellis Award from the Crime Writers of Canada, and was shortlisted for the Guardian Award in Great Britain. His most recent young adult novel, *A Thief in the*

House of Memory, made the Best Book lists of both *Publishers Weekly* and *Kirkus.* He lives with his wife, Amanda West Lewis, in Perth, Ontario. His three grown children live in London, Halifax, and Toronto. To learn more about Tim, visit www.timwynne-jones.com.

Editor Ann Angel has written biographies for educational markets but has focused on her true obsession, young adult fiction, since graduating in 1999 from Vermont College's MFA in Writing for Children and Young Adults program. She has taught as a writer/counselor for the National Book Foundation's summer writing program and teaches journalism and creative writing at Mount Mary College in Milwaukee, where she lives with her husband and whichever of her four young adult kids happen to be home. Ann defines beauty as "family, friends, and sometimes even strangers connecting in a meaningful way. It is the way writers, both new and known, joined together out of friendship and mentoring to bring their beautiful art into the world for this book." Visit Ann at www.annangelwriter.com.

This book was designed and art directed by Chad W. Beckerman. The text is set in 12-point Adobe Garamond, a typeface that is based on those created in the sixteenth century by Claude Garamond. Garamond modeled his typefaces on those created by Venetian printers at the end of the fifteenth century. The modern version used in this book was designed by Robert Slimbach, who studied Garamond's historic typefaces at the Plantin-Moretus Museum in Antwerp, Belgium. The display type is York-Script and Futura.